THE NEW. FAMOUS FIVE

FIVE AND THE FORGOTTEN TREASURE

Inspired by *Enid Blyton*

THE NEW FAMOUS FIVE

FIVE AND THE FORGOTTEN TREASURE

CHRIS SMITH

Illustrated by James Lancett

HODDER CHILDREN'S BOOKS
First published in Great Britain in 2025 by Hodder & Stoughton Limited

5 7 9 10 8 6 4

The Famous Five®, Enid Blyton® and Enid Blyton's signature are
registered trade marks of Hodder & Stoughton Limited
Text copyright © Chris Smith, 2025
Illustrations by James Lancett. Illustrations copyright © Hodder & Stoughton Limited, 2025

A CIP catalogue record for this book is available from the British Library.

ISBN: 978 1 444 97872 8

Printed and bound in Great Britain by Clays Ltd, Elcograf S.p.A.

The paper and board used in this book
are made from wood from responsible sources.

MIX
Paper | Supporting
responsible forestry
FSC® C104740

Hodder Children's Books
An imprint of Hachette Children's Group
Part of Hodder & Stoughton Limited
Carmelite House
50 Victoria Embankment
London EC4Y 0DZ

The authorised representative in the EEA is Hachette Ireland,
8 Castlecourt Centre, Dublin 15, D15 XTP3, Ireland (email: info@hbgi.ie)

An Hachette UK Company
www.hachette.co.uk
www.hachettechildrens.co.uk

To those who know that, down the path,

Or just beyond the hill,

Across the waves or in the caves,

Behind a door, across the moor . . .

There is adventure still.

Contents

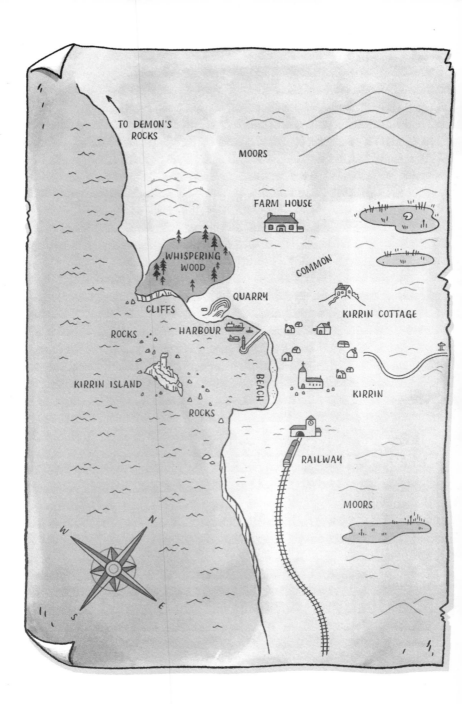

The Train to Kirrin

With a shriek of its whistle, the train burst from the tunnel in a cloud of steam and began to rattle round a long, shallow bend in the track. In the front carriage, bright sunlight reflected from green fields cast dancing shadows across the faces of three children and a dog, all gazing eagerly out of the window. Excitement was building up all along the train like an electrical charge until finally a little girl near the front of the carriage let out a yell, 'There it is! I can see it! Look!' In the middle distance, between two low hills, the sea had appeared, glittering and dazzling blue beneath a cloudless summer sky.

'Kirrin station! Kirrin, our next and final stop!' announced a red-faced conductor, rolling from side to side as he made his way between the seats. 'We shall be arriving at Kirrin station in five minutes!'

As the train began to slow down, the view of the seaside filled the windows along the left-hand side. Sailing boats and a faraway cargo ship dotted the water, and bright yellow gorse bushes flashed past. Adults began to rummage in the luggage rack for bags, buckets and spades and picnic baskets and chattering families filled the aisle as, at last, the train pulled into a smart little station with the word KIRRIN picked out on a freshly painted sign. From outside came another short, sharp blast on the engine's whistle and the dog – a black and white Border collie – gave a startled 'Wuff!'

'Isn't it *gorgeous?*' asked one woman, holding up a digital camera to take a picture through the train window. 'So lovely that they still run the steam trains, isn't it? You really feel like you're back in the 1940s!'

'Come on, Mum!' her son called out from the end of the carriage. 'Don't stand there taking photos all day! I want an ice cream!'

The three children and their dog waited until the crowd had died down before making their way on to the platform. The oldest of the three – a girl with short, dark hair and keen eyes behind black glasses – paused and rummaged in a pocket of the rucksack she carried. 'Hold on, Tom!' she called to her younger brother, who was following the crowd towards the exit. 'I've got a map here somewhere! Don't rush off before we know where we're going!'

Tom stopped and turned, grinning. 'But I heard someone say ice cream!' he called. 'We can look at the boring map after we've had some. Come on, Maddy,' he pleaded, taking a few steps back towards his sister. 'We're supposed to be on holiday!'

'Wait for Fran, at least,' Maddy told him. Behind her, their sister – the middle of the children in age – was struggling down from the carriage carrying a large suitcase on wheels with the collie scampering and barking around her legs. Fran was the tallest of the three, with long dark hair and a serious expression.

'Be patient, Gilbert!' she told the excited dog sternly. 'This bag's full of your stuff, after all!'

'What have you got for him in there – a whole kennel or something?' asked her brother. 'We're gonna get ice cream! Hurry up before bossy-boots Maddy changes her mind!'

'Oi!' His eldest sister laughed.

'Isn't anyone going to meet us at the station?' asked Fran, finally wrestling her suitcase on to the platform and looking around at the thinning crowd. 'How will we know where to go?'

'Grandad printed out a map for me,' Maddy told her reassuringly. 'And he told me exactly where to go. Kirrin's not a big place. We'll find our way easily once we've fed Tom an ice cream, so he stops whingeing!'

'I have not whinged even a little bit!' Tom protested. 'Just saying – it would be a crime to come to the seaside and not have an ice cream immediately, right? Everyone knows that's the rule. Even Gilbert agrees, don't you, boy? Eh?'

Gilbert gave a delighted 'Woof!' and scampered up to Tom, who scratched him behind the ears.

'Come on then,' said Maddy, shouldering her rucksack and leading her brother and sister towards a white wooden gate with EXIT painted on it in bright red letters.

A wide, curved street sloped gently down from the station towards the seafront, and it seemed like the whole trainload of people was heading in the same direction. Skipping children with buckets and snapping parents with cameras filled the sunlit pavement, lined with smart little houses and shops. As the three rounded a bend, the sea came back into view and they all stopped. 'Wow!' Tom exclaimed. 'Grandad was right! It really is an amazing place!'

'Look! There's the island!' said Fran, pointing far out in the bay where an island was surrounded by sharp rocks jutting out of the water. 'And the castle! Just like he said!' One high tower and several ruined walls were visible among the trees, with a cloud of black birds circling above.

'Ruined castles are cool,' Tom declared, 'but I want to see the beach first! Come on!' Together, the children carried on into the town, following a wide cobbled promenade along the seafront. Fish and chip shops and ice cream parlours lined one side of it, along with shops selling beach toys, seashells and souvenirs. Double doors opened into a dark open space called JIM'S AMUSEMENTS, filled with bleeping, flashing games machines.

Tom, with Gilbert still gambolling at his heels, led the way to a wide shopfront declaring that it contained SANDERS' ORIGINAL ICE CREAM. HANDMADE AT THE OLDEST DAIRY IN KIRRIN. 'Clotted coconut cream . . . hazelnut caramel twist . . . strawberry shortbread chunk . . .' he read, peering into a glass cabinet filled with tubs. 'I'll have to try every single one! How long are we here for?'

'Two weeks,' replied Maddy, looking around her and smiling as they paid for their cones. It was only mid-morning, but the pale yellow sands of Kirrin beach were already full of brightly coloured umbrellas and stripy windbreaks.

* * *

The children strolled along the front to the far end of the beach, licking their ice creams, and stopped next to a wooden signboard advertising trips around Kirrin Bay that was leaning against a stone harbour wall. A smart, freshly painted boat was waiting nearby. Maddy dropped her rucksack to the ground and pulled a printed page from the top pocket. 'Right, let's see where we're going, shall we?' She sat down on the low wall to concentrate and squinted at the paper in the bright sunlight.

'We want to land on the island,' a loud, confident voice announced nearby. An expensively dressed man and his family were talking to the boat's owner, who had a shock of white hair and a sunburnt, weather-beaten face.

'Kirrin Island is private,' said the old fisherman apologetically. 'No landing allowed.'

'Oh, come on,' said the man, reaching into his trouser pocket for a well-stuffed wallet. 'I'm sure if we make it worth your while . . .'

'The owner's a very old friend of mine,' replied the fisherman, looking down at the wallet with a small smile. 'A *very* old friend. And there isn't enough money in there, or any wallet in the world, to change that. I'll take your family for a nice trip around the bay,' he went on, looking the bossy man straight in the eye, 'but nobody lands on Kirrin Island without permission. It's protected, see?'

Fran looked out across the water at the island with new interest. It looked like a wonderful place, with its ruined castle and rocky shores. Gilbert gave a small bark. 'I know,' she told her dog. 'I wish we could go there too. But you heard what the man said. No landing without permission. I wonder who the mysterious owner is?'

'I think we're heading in the right direction,' said Maddy, breaking into Fran's musings. She pointed at the page in her hand. 'It says to walk along the seafront until we reach the harbour wall. Head right, along the road that leads uphill towards the common . . .' She pointed away from the sea to where a heather-covered hillside rose above the back of the small town. Beyond was a mass of dark woodland, spreading up a high headland and towards the cliffs that stood to one side of the bay. 'Then it just says to ask anyone where to go.'

She frowned. 'Grandad's written here, "Anyone in the town will know where to find Kirrin Cottage."'

'Kirrin Cottage?' echoed a voice. The family had moved off, and the fisherman was leaning on the rail of his boat, watching them keenly. 'You off to see the professor, are you?'

'That's right,' Maddy told him politely. 'Do you know where it is?'

'I should say I do,' he replied, his kind, crinkly eyes taking in the three children. 'Been a while since any children have gone looking for Kirrin Cottage, though. Straight up the hill, there' – he pointed – 'and as you come to the very edge of the town, it's the large white house on the left. You can't miss it.'

'Thanks!' Maddy shouldered her rucksack and led the way.

'Give my best to the prof!' shouted the fisherman after them. 'And mind you're on your best behaviour!' He chuckled as he turned back to his boat.

'I wonder what he means by that,' said Fran nervously as they trudged up the hill away from the beach. 'Best behaviour? What's that all about?'

'Yeah!' agreed Tom. 'We're supposed to be on holiday. Nobody wants to be *behaving*!' Gilbert gave another 'Wuff' of agreement.

'It's some relative of ours, right?' Fran asked Maddy. 'Do you know anything about who they are? I don't like the sound of them so far.'

'A distant relative,' said Maddy as the sounds of the busy beach faded behind them. 'I think a cousin twice removed or something? But Grandad wouldn't tell me much more. Said he wanted it to be a surprise.' Maddy stopped at a fork in the road, studying the paper again.

'Let me see.' Fran came to join her, taking the printed map from her sister. 'It's that way,' she said, pointing up the steeper of the two streets. 'Wait a minute,' she went on, turning it over. 'What's he written here?' On the back of the map were a couple of lines of small, cramped handwriting.

'I hadn't seen that!' Maddy squinted over Fran's shoulder to make out the spidery words. 'Two last pieces of advice,' she slowly read out loud. 'Firstly, no sudden loud noises.'

'Well, this professor's sounding like all kinds of fun already,' said Tom sarcastically, finishing off the last piece of his ice cream cone. 'Best behaviour *and* no loud noises. Great!'

'And secondly,' Maddy went on, frowning in puzzlement, 'if you want her to answer you . . . don't EVER call her "Georgina".'

2

The Professor

The wide street led up a steep slope out of town, with the green common and the dark woods at the very top of the hill looming over the houses. It was a hot day, and the children and Gilbert were soon panting and sweating. 'It can't be much further, can it?' protested Tom, shifting his sports bag from one hand to the other. 'I'm starving! Lunch better be on the table when we get there.'

'You *just* had a massive ice cream,' Fran told him.

'Erm, ice creams don't count as food,' Tom pointed out. 'This is well known!'

'Look!' said Maddy, stopping. 'That must be it!'

Right at the edge of the town of Kirrin was a very old-looking house of white-painted stone. It stood in a wide garden with tall trees and a well-tended vegetable patch and was much bigger than their own terraced house in a crowded city.

'Cottage?' muttered Tom to himself. 'More like Kirrin Mansion!'

As the children approached the cottage, they could hear the sound of raised voices and after a few seconds there was the sharp slamming of a door. A man came stomping down the path through the front garden, muttering angrily to himself under his breath. He had straggly dark hair that brushed his collar and, despite the heat of the day, was wearing a long raincoat that swished around his legs.

A scruffy-looking dog followed at his heels and Gilbert, catching sight of it, gave a delighted bark and bounded over, wagging his tail enthusiastically. The man gave a start and cried out in alarm. 'Get away!' he snarled, kicking out with one of his muddy black boots. Gilbert, thinking it was a game, darted back and crouched down with his front legs stuck out, ready to play. But the man's own dog cowered behind with its tail between his legs.

'Sorry if he startled you,' said Fran coolly, bending down to grab Gilbert's collar and pulling him away. 'He only wanted to say hello,' she said reassuringly to the brown and white dog. 'He wasn't going to hurt you.' It gave a weak wag of its tail.

'Out of my way,' said the man impatiently, brushing past them and out into the road.

'Do you know if this is the right place to find the professor?' called Maddy after him as he stalked away downhill towards the seafront with his dog trotting gloomily after him.

'You won't find anything you're looking for in there,' he snapped back over his shoulder before rounding the corner and vanishing from view.

The three children looked at each other with raised eyebrows.

'Well,' said Tom, 'I can confidently say that this summer holiday is not scoring high on the fun scale so far.'

'I wonder who he was,' said Fran curiously, staring down the hill after the rude man. She had always found that dogs tended to mirror their owners, and the downtrodden air of the mongrel that was following him made her feel somehow sad for them both.

Maddy, though, had more urgent things to worry about: where was this professor they were supposed to be staying with, and why did everybody seem to be so afraid of her? Feeling determined, she led the way towards the green-painted front door. Tom and Fran followed, looking around the garden. There were several wooden sheds along the back wall, and chickens scratched and fluffed their wings in a large, wire-covered run. But other than their contented clucks, there was no sound. Kirrin Cottage seemed silent and deserted. Maddy raised her hand and knocked three times on the door.

For a long moment, nothing happened. Then, from somewhere inside the house, there came the distant sound of a door being pulled sharply open. 'I've told you already – GO AWAY!' shouted a muffled voice.

And, with that, there was the sound of the door slamming closed again.

Maddy, Fran and Tom all took a step backwards in alarm. Even Gilbert sat back uncertainly on his haunches with a small whimper. The three children turned to stare at each other. 'Told you,' Tom said solemnly. 'Worst. Holiday. Ever.'

'What are we supposed to do now?' asked Fran in alarm, looking pale and worried. 'We're supposed to stay here! Where are we going to sleep?'

'Calm down,' Maddy told her, straightening her shoulders. Her younger sister tended to get anxious, and she knew that at times like these she needed to act older than her eleven years. 'Come on,' she told Fran and Tom. 'Let's go round the back. Perhaps there's somebody else who'll be more friendly.'

'Who?' said Tom.

'I dunno,' Maddy replied, still trying to sound braver than she felt. 'Like, a gardener or something.' She led the others round the side of Kirrin Cottage, towards the wooden outhouses which stood behind the neatly tended vegetable patch.

'Oh, look!' said Fran, pointing at a large painted wooden kennel beside one of the sheds. 'I wonder if there's another dog here!'

But as they rounded the corner, all three children stopped and stared. The back of Kirrin Cottage looked over a wide lawn and a dry-stone wall separated it from the steeply sloping moorland. But this was no ordinary garden. Right in the middle was a strange metal structure. It looked a bit like a miniature electricity pylon, with a nest of wires sticking out at the top. A thick tangle of cables led from the base of the tower, snaking across the lawn and through an open window at the back of the house.

'What the . . .' began Maddy, but before she could say any more, there was a deep humming from somewhere inside, and the wires at the top of the small pylon began to glow and quiver. A buzzing noise like a giant beehive filled the garden. Then, suddenly, there was a sharp flash of light from the wires and a pop from inside the open window, followed by a wisp of bright white smoke. A voice cried out in frustration: 'Blast it!'

All three children had automatically ducked, Fran

shielding Gilbert's face with her hands. As they straightened up, blinking and with starbursts clouding their vision, the window opened wider and someone climbed nimbly out into the garden, coughing and fanning their hands in front of their face.

'Are you all right?' asked Fran straight away, moving towards them.

'Who are you? What are you doing here? Stay back!' barked the figure.

As the smoke cleared, the children could see a tall person dressed in jeans and an old, tatty sweater. A pair of piercingly bright blue eyes glared at them from beneath a mop of short, curly grey hair.

'Are you the professor?' questioned Maddy, following her sister.

'Well, let's look at the evidence,' said Tom quietly behind her. 'Crazy exploding experiment? Check. Scary angry person? Check. Yep, I think on balance that's probably the professor.'

'Don't go near the wires!' the individual was now warning Maddy, who was walking forward with her hand outstretched. 'I won't,' Maddy promised. 'So –

are you the professor? Weren't you expecting us?' She stopped, still holding out her hand.

'I'm not expecting anybody!' came the angry reply. 'And I'm in the middle of a vital part of my experiment! I can't have all these interruptions! People knocking on the door constantly, day and night, and then a bunch of kids showing up in the garden. It's insufferable!'

'Not sure she's gonna shake your hand, Maddy,' called out Tom cheerfully. Slowly, his sister lowered her arm to her side, but she wasn't giving up.

'We've come to stay with you. Our grandfather arranged it. He says you've exchanged several emails. I'm Maddy, by the way. And you must be Professor Kirrin,' she persisted, having made up her mind not to be intimidated by this rather scary person.

'Emails?' said the professor. 'Grandfather? What on earth are you talking about? I haven't had any emails from any grandfather. And I certainly haven't agreed to have a load of children here, messing around and interrupting my experiments! As if!'

'*Are* you Professor Kirrin?' Maddy pressed on.

'Professor Georgina Kirrin . . .' The blue eyes narrowed in anger, and she remembered the note her grandfather had scribbled. 'I mean,' she corrected herself quickly, '*George*. Are you George?'

For a split second, the professor's face cleared. 'Who told you to call me that?' she asked suspiciously.

'Our grandfather,' repeated Maddy patiently.

'His name's Richard Kirrin,' Fran broke in.

'But we call him Grandad Dick,' added Tom.

'Dick?' The professor looked at them in astonishment. 'You're Dick's grandkids? What on earth are you doing here? Has something happened to him?'

'No.' Maddy was hoping that this mysterious professor wasn't quite as fierce or as absent-minded as she appeared at first. 'We've come to stay with you. He set it up with you by email.'

'E . . . MAIL,' reinforced Tom, as if he was talking to someone very, very old. 'Like letters . . . only on a COMPUTER. You know?'

'Think you're funny, do you?' growled the professor at him. 'Yes, you take after your grandad, all right. He was always the joker.'

'So you *do* remember?' asked Maddy with a sigh of relief.

'I can't think straight,' complained Professor George Kirrin. 'Knocking on the door in the middle of my vital test, then popping up in the back garden like jack-in-the-boxes! How am I supposed to work?'

'But we can stay, right?' asked Fran nervously. Her anxious brain had been full of visions of sleeping on the beach.

'Doesn't look as if I have much choice, does it?' George reached up and wiped her eyes, which were red and sore-looking from the smoke that was still eddying from the open window. 'You'll have to leave me in peace, though. I'm right on the edge of a breakthrough.' She gestured towards the metal structure that was still fizzing faintly, before turning sharply and heading towards the back door. As the children moved to follow her, she caught sight of Gilbert trailing after Fran. 'Not the dog!' said George sharply, a pained expression shooting across her face.

'What? But . . .' Fran looked over her shoulder in

surprise towards the smart red kennel in the garden. Surely this was a house where dogs were welcome?

'He stays outside,' the professor said firmly, marching to the back door. 'I don't care for dogs.'

Fran wasn't sure, but she thought she heard George quietly add, 'Not any more,' as she disappeared inside Kirrin Cottage.

3

A Noise in the Dark

Coming in from the bright sunshine, it took the children's eyes a moment to adjust to the dim light. The back door led on to a wide hallway paved with pale stone. Coats and umbrellas were hung behind the door above a jumble of muddy boots. The day was already hot, but inside Kirrin Cottage it felt calm and cool. George stood waiting for them, hands on her hips.

'Right. Ground rules,' she said, her blue eyes staring them down. 'You know rule one already: my name is George.'

Tom stuck his thumbs up to say 'message received'. From what he'd seen of her so far, he certainly didn't think it would be a good idea to get on the professor's bad side. Although, looking at her grumpy face, he wasn't sure she had any other side to get on.

'Rule two,' George went on, pointing to a stout wooden door on their left, from beneath which a small tendril of smoke was curling. 'That's my study. Nobody goes in there, under any circumstances, ever, not for any reason. Got it?'

'Got it,' agreed Maddy, also feeling it was better to try and make friends as far as possible. They were staying there for two whole weeks, after all.

'Can I ask a question?' said Fran. She had reluctantly told Gilbert to 'Stay!' before coming inside, but she felt sure he wouldn't really be forced to live in the garden for the whole holiday.

'Rule three: no questions,' George snapped. 'Now, follow me.' She led the way along the hall to a large dining room and a sitting room with comfortable armchairs and a fireplace. Neither looked as if they were used much. At the far end of the hallway, through an arch, was a wide kitchen with a long wooden table at the centre. High windows looked out across the town and the sea, with Kirrin Island visible in the distance.

'Don't bother me and I won't bother you,' said George as she led them beneath the archway.

'She's a right bundle of laughs, isn't she?' whispered Tom to Fran, who gave an accidental snort of laughter.

'I know what children these days are like,' George said, scowling at them both. 'Think everything's a big joke. Expect to have it all done for them. Well, there's none of that here, got it?'

'No jokes, said Tom solemnly, elbowing Fran in the ribs. 'No things being done for us. Got it.'

George gave him a long, suspicious look.

'We won't get in your way,' Maddy promised seriously. 'Honest. We'll be more than happy to take care of ourselves.'

'Good,' said George, eyeing her with a slight twitch of her mouth. 'Now, I expect you're hungry. Children are always hungry, aren't they? Your grandad certainly always was.' Her blue eyes seemed to look far away for a moment before she opened the door to a well-stocked larder. Clearly, even though she'd since forgotten, she must have known that the children were coming to stay. The shelves were stacked with packets of biscuits and a large sponge cake stood on a stand underneath a glass cover. In the big double fridge were packs of cooked chicken drumsticks, pork pies and containers of cheeses and salads.

Five minutes later, the scrubbed wooden table was piled with food. Much of it seemed to be homemade – including a couple of jars that George had pulled from a cupboard and dumped in front of them.

'What's this one?' Tom wanted to know, picking one up. 'There's no label on it.'

'Never been much of a fan of labels,' said George.

'It's pickled onions,' Fran told him, twisting off the lid and sniffing.

'So, it's definitely OK to stay?' asked Maddy. After the very unusual welcome they'd received, she wanted to make double sure. She kept half expecting this peculiar professor to change her mind and throw them back out into the street.

'Said so, didn't I?' replied George gruffly. 'Food's in the kitchen. Bedrooms are upstairs. Beach is over there.' She pointed out of the window. 'And make sure you clear up the kitchen.' Without another word, she swept out of the room and a moment later they heard the study door slam shut.

'Just like I said,' Tom told the others, popping a pickled onion in his mouth. 'Worst holiday ever.'

'Are you kidding?' said Maddy, looking out towards the shimmering sea. 'A whole fortnight with no grown-ups to bother us? A mysterious old house, a kitchen stocked with food and a brilliant beach right on our doorstep? BEST holiday ever! Come on, let's eat, get this tidied away and hit the arcade!'

Gilbert gave a delighted bark when Fran reappeared at the back door, hoping she might be bringing him a sausage roll.

'Shut that dog up!' came George's angry voice through the open study window.

'Don't mind that grumpy old professor,' Fran told him, kneeling to run her hands through his silky fur.

'I won't make you sleep out in the cold garden. Now, come on – we're going to the beach!'

Maddy, Tom and Fran spent a happy afternoon exploring the little seaside town of Kirrin. They spent ages in the arcade before Tom dragged his sisters back out into the sunshine. Maddy bought a bright red ball from one of the stalls along the seafront and they played a long game of football right along the beach, dodging feasting families and tottering toddlers, and occasionally wading in to retrieve the ball from the sea after a shot went wide. Finally, as day-trippers started to stream back up the hill towards the railway station, the children bought fish and chips from a van and ate them out of the paper, sitting on the same low wall they had rested on that morning. Seagulls wheeled just above their heads and prowled nearby hoping to peck up a stray chip, but Gilbert was on patrol and made sure they kept a safe distance away. He wasn't giving up his right to any food the children didn't want.

There was no sign of George when they finally climbed back up the hill to Kirrin Cottage that evening, when the summer sky was turning a deep burnished gold. Maddy crept close to the firmly shut study door and thought she could hear the faint tapping of computer keys. 'She must be working on her big scientific breakthrough,' she told Fran and Tom with a smile. 'Come on, let's find our beds. I'm wiped.'

'What about Gilbert?' Fran asked her as they grabbed the bags that they had dumped by the back door earlier. 'He doesn't really need to stay outside, does he?'

'It's nice and warm,' Maddy reassured her sister, seeing her anguished expression. 'And he sleeps downstairs at home so he won't miss you. There's a kennel and everything. Just for tonight, at least. Maybe if we get on George's good side for a day or two, he'll be allowed inside.'

Reluctantly, Fran led Gilbert to the kennel. He lay down on his tummy, looking up at her with sad eyes. 'It's not my decision,' she told him softly. Then she glanced back at the house, towards the open study window and the wires leading out towards the metal tower. 'Look, just wait until that weird professor has gone to sleep and then I'll come and get you, OK? She can't stay up all night fiddling with her silly experiments.'

Gilbert's tail wagged energetically as if he understood exactly what she was saying.

Upstairs, the children found two bedrooms towards the front of the house. They had sloping ceilings, neatly made beds ready in each, and the girls' room had a window with a view out across Kirrin Bay. 'This is awesome!' said Maddy, sitting down on the bed nearest the window and bouncing. 'We'll keep the window open to let in some sea air.'

'How come you get the best view?' Tom wanted to know. His room was larger, but the window looked over the outhouses at the side of the house rather than towards the beach.

'Because we're older, obviously,' Maddy told him with a grin. 'Now, come on. Get ready for bed and go to sleep. We can head down for a swim before breakfast.'

Half an hour later, as the darkness of a summer night finally gathered around Kirrin Cottage, there was no sound in the two bedrooms except for quiet breathing. Tom and Maddy were both fast asleep. But Fran was not. She turned from side to side and sat up every time she felt herself drifting towards sleep, waiting to hear the slam of the study door and the professor's footsteps coming up the stairs to bed. She was determined to rescue poor Gilbert from spending the whole night outside.

Finally, when another hour had passed and owls had begun to call in the woods at the top of the hill, Fran made up her mind. George must have fallen asleep downstairs or gone to bed early before they'd come back from the beach. Maybe they'd imagined the noise of her computer. Besides, the air flowing through the open window was now cool, and the thought of Gilbert out in the kennel was unbearable. She sat up sideways and quickly pulled on her jacket and trainers. Silently, she crept to the door and listened. Apart from the slow ticking of the large grandfather clock in the hall, the house seemed completely still. She began to creep softly down the staircase.

Just then, there was a sharp cry from downstairs, followed by a crash and a dull thump. Without stopping to think, Fran leapt down the rest of the stairs two at a time to see what was going on.

The Shadow of the Past

Once she reached the bottom of the stairs, Fran stopped and listened once again. For a moment she considered running back up the stairs and waking Maddy. But her older sister might think she was making a fuss about nothing. After all, she told herself, old houses like this were full of strange sounds. Perhaps she'd heard nothing more than a clunk in the old heating pipes, or the professor moving about downstairs. But a voice deep inside was telling her that something was very, very wrong. Ignoring the anxious prickling between her shoulder blades, she tiptoed towards the study door where she felt sure the strange noise had come from. Fran pushed down the brass handle and, with a loud snick, the heavy door swung smoothly open.

George's study was the largest room in Kirrin Cottage. It stretched across most of the back edge of the house, with twin sets of high windows. These were both thrown wide open; cool night air and bright moonlight spilt through – so bright that for a moment Fran was convinced that a lamp must have been left on somewhere. She stepped gingerly just inside the door and looked around.

A painting hung above the wide fireplace, almost covering a series of wooden panels set into the wall. It showed a dark, hulking shipwreck thrown up on to a rocky shore, with threatening clouds boiling overhead. The stormy, mysterious scene suited the owner of this room perfectly. To her right, away from the windows, was a wall entirely filled with bookshelves, crammed with books, boxes, framed pictures on stands and other strange objects. A golden medal was set in an elaborate frame above the words: *Fallonian Order of Merit. Awarded for the recovery of the Crown Jewels of Fallonia.* Sitting on the same shelf was a leather collar set with metal studs. Fran frowned. If George didn't like dogs, why on earth would she have a kennel and a collar?

Another noise made Fran freeze in fright. Over near the windows was an enormous, cluttered wooden desk. A computer sat on one end, beside a giant jumble of papers and notebooks. And, from behind this desk, there came a long, deep groan. Forcing herself to move despite her terror, Fran approached, stepping on to the patterned rug that spread out in front of the fireplace to cover most of the floor. She gasped. Two scuffed brown boots were sticking out – someone was lying on the floor underneath the window.

Instinctively, Fran darted forward to help. There, stretched out on the wooden floorboards, was George. She sat up slightly and groaned again, squinting at Fran in the moonlight. 'What?' she said groggily. 'How . . . ?' Then, suddenly, her eyes widened. 'Watch out! Behind you!'

And then several things happened almost all at once.

The door had swung closed, revealing a man who had been hiding behind it. He was already halfway across the room, moving towards Fran with a savage look on his face. In that split second she recognised him. It was the scruffy-looking man who had been coming down the garden when they had first arrived at Kirrin Cottage. Fran caught a glint in the moonlight as the man lifted his arm and saw that he was holding a short, heavy wooden club. But before he could reach her, there was a deep growl from the open window. Gilbert was poised on the sill, teeth bared, having sensed danger. He gave a great leap into the room, clearing the desk, and knocked into the man's chest, bowling him over backwards. The man fell on to the hearth rug with a cry of pain.

There was a thunder of footsteps from the staircase. Maddy and Tom had been awoken by the voices and were stampeding down to investigate. 'Who's down here?' Maddy was calling in her bossiest big-sister voice. 'What's going on?'

'In here! Quick!' Fran shouted. If she'd had time to think, she might have sent her sister and brother off to get help, but she was in a panic. They came bundling into the study to be greeted by the sight of the man spread-eagled on the rug with a growling Gilbert on his chest. Fran, looking pale and scared in the moonlight, was over by the desk with George struggling to stand nearby.

'Hold him down!' shouted George desperately, but it was too late. With a snarl, the straggly-haired man had thrown Gilbert off his chest. The dog rolled away with a howl of pain. The man struggled to his knees, swishing his club menacingly at Maddy and Tom.

'Over by the fireplace!' he ordered. 'All of you! Now! And keep that dog with you or you'll regret it!'

'Here, Gilbert! Quick!' called Fran, as she helped George to her feet and joined the others by the fireplace.

'He must have sneaked in while I was working on the test results!' said George groggily. 'He knocked me out!'

'No talking!' The man waved his cudgel threateningly. There was a whine from behind him and, for the first time, the children noticed that his sad-looking dog was cowering behind the door. 'Shut up,' said the man angrily. The dog whimpered unhappily and both Fran and George gave furious growls. Neither of them could stand people who weren't kind to animals.

'I already told you yesterday,' George grumbled. 'You're not getting that map! I'll never give it up!'

'Is he after your experiments?' asked Maddy, putting an arm around Tom and Fran.

The man gave a coarse, crowing laugh. 'Experiments!' he echoed scornfully. 'Of course I'm not after her experiments. Her father couldn't get them to work and neither can *Georgina*.'

'Shut up!' snapped George furiously. 'How dare you talk about my father!' Her eyes rested on a silver-framed photograph on the desk. It showed a severe-looking man with thick eyebrows and a full head of dark, wavy hair.

'Well, what does he want then?' Fran sounded scared.

'*Georgina* knows very well what I want,' said the man in a mocking tone of voice.

'It's *George*,' corrected Maddy crossly. The professor might be fierce and grumpy, but after all she was family – even if only a distant cousin. And she felt annoyed by the way this man kept using the wrong name deliberately.

'You wouldn't want these kids to get hurt now, would you?' pressed the man, lifting his club high.

'You wouldn't!' gasped George.

'Oh, yes I would,' he told her, licking his lips nervously and glancing out of the window. 'I told you earlier – I've got nothing to lose any more. I'm . . . I'm desperate. So give me that sea chart! NOW! Or I won't be responsible for what happens.' His voice sounded strange, as if he was stuck halfway between fury and desperate panic.

'All right, all right!' George held up her hands, palms outwards. 'Just calm down for a moment. Don't hurt the children. I'll give you the chart, OK? Then you can get out of here and leave me alone!'

'Who is he?' squeaked Tom in a small, frightened voice. 'I'm scared!' Gilbert gave an angry growl, and Fran knelt to grab his collar.

'Stay calm,' George told Tom, patting him on the shoulder. 'This will all be over in a moment, don't worry. He's just a coward,' she added with a scornful look at the man. 'Nobody to get worked up about.' She walked slowly to the desk and pulled open a wide, shallow drawer. It was filled with sheets of thick paper, and George flicked through these before pulling out one sheet and handing it to the man. He cast his eyes across it greedily. It was old and yellowed, with deep crease marks across it.

'This is it,' he muttered to himself. 'There's the island . . . the rocks and . . . *yes. There!* Breathing hard, he folded up the chart and stuffed it inside his jacket.

'Now,' said George, rejoining the others on the rug, 'you've got what you want. Get out of my house!'

'Oh, yes,' said the man, glaring. 'You'd like that, wouldn't you? To be left in peace so you can go straight to the police! I don't think so!' He marched to the window and sent a sharp whisper out into the moonlit garden. 'Clay! I've got it!'

There was the sound of soft footsteps across the grass, and a new face appeared at the window. Unlike the straggle-haired man, he gave no hint of desperation or panic. Instead, he had a shark-like air of stillness and cold danger. His unusual, pale eyes assessed the children and George without blinking, before he looked down and adjusted the cuffs of his sharp grey suit.

'Well, what are you waiting for?' he asked in a soft, chilling tone, charged with menace.

'I can't do anything until daylight, can I?' whined the man.

Fran, watching him, thought he looked just as defeated as his own dog and remembered the way it had slunk sadly after him the previous day

Clay gave a short sigh. 'Very well,' he said. 'In that case, Professor, you and your young companions will have to stay here until our friend fetches what he owes me. You have twenty-four hours – and you know better than to try and cheat me a second time, I hope.'

'I'll get it for you, Clay,' replied the man, slinking to the window. 'I said so, didn't I?' With his dog following, he climbed out into the night and vanished.

'Make yourselves comfortable,' the cold-eyed man told George and the children in his soft voice. 'And I strongly advise you not to try and escape.' He patted a bulge inside his suit jacket. 'I have a better weapon in here than a wooden stick. Your telephone has been disabled, and my associates and I will be watching the house from all sides.' He gave a brief glance towards the window, and in the moonlight they could make out the shapes of two more people out by the garden wall.

'This will all be over soon,' the man reassured them calmly. 'Don't cause me any trouble and you won't get hurt. You can go back to your little experiments as soon as he finds the treasure.'

5

Secret Passages and
Sunken Treasure

After the man called Clay vanished back into the darkness of the garden, Maddy was the first to break the silence. 'Treasure?' she breathed. 'What did he mean, treasure?'

'That's what you're focussing on?' said Tom a little shakily. 'The word "treasure"? Not the fact that we've just been threatened by some bloke with what seems to be an actual gun?'

George, meanwhile, had darted over to the window, crouched down and was peering out across the garden. 'Looks like they meant what they said,' she whispered.

'One of them is watching from the back wall. Another one's gone round the side. Looks like the house is covered so, once I've gone, don't get any ideas about going outside, all right? Just sit tight and wait for me.'

'Wait for you?' said Maddy, shocked. 'What do you mean? Where do you think you're going?'

'To stop them from getting hold of the treasure,' the professor replied in a matter-of-fact tone.

'On your own?'

'Of course, on my own. Who's going to help me?' George looked around the study at the children with her usual frown in place. 'You lot?'

'Why shouldn't we help?' retorted Maddy, stung.

'Don't make me laugh,' George replied. 'Children these days aren't cut out for adventures. They just sit on their backsides watching TV all day.' She gave a short, scornful laugh.

'What a load of complete rubbish!' Everybody turned in surprise to look at Fran. She had been kneeling on the hearth rug comforting Gilbert. But when she had heard George's words she had got to her feet, her face blazing.

'I beg your pardon?' said George, her face like thunder.

'I said,' repeated Fran furiously, 'you're talking a load of complete rubbish. "Kids these days not being cut out for adventures." As *if*. The world might have changed since you were going off recovering stolen crown jewels' – she waved towards the framed medal on the shelves – 'but kids haven't changed. It's not our fault you got old and grumpy. If you don't want our help, that's fine. But don't you *dare* say we're not brave enough.'

George Kirrin listened to this speech with a curious expression on her face, staring hard at Fran for several long seconds in the moonlight. Then, suddenly, she broke into a wide grin. 'OK, OK,' she told the children. 'I admit it – I might have been wrong. You know something, Fran? You actually remind me of somebody I used to know a long time ago.'

'Who's that?' asked Fran, still breathing hard and red in the face with anger.

'Me,' replied George. 'Fine – if you want to help me, then I'd be glad to have you. Ready for an adventure?'

'I'm not sure I remember signing up for an adventure,' said Tom in a slightly shaky voice. 'I was more planning on going back to the beach and eating a lot more ice cream.'

'You don't choose whether or not to have an adventure,' said George firmly. 'Some people just walk into adventures all the time. That's what your grandfather told me once, anyway.' And then, to everyone's surprise, she knelt down on the rug and threw her arms around Gilbert. 'Weren't you brave, hey?' she told him, ruffling his ears. 'Aren't you a good boy?'

Gilbert, delighted, began to lick her face all over.

'What can we do, though?' asked Maddy practically. 'We're trapped! You said it yourself – those men are watching the front and back of the house. We'll have to stay here!'

'Oh no, we won't!' replied George, getting back to her feet. 'I've never done what people told me to my whole life – and I'm certainly not going to start now! You,' she pointed to Tom, 'go into the kitchen and fill a bag with as much food as you can.

There are plenty of rucksacks hanging in the hall. You two,' she indicated to Maddy and Fran, 'grab a few clothes for all three of you. I'll get sleeping bags and camping gear. Be back here in ten minutes. We're escaping.'

'But they're watching the doors!' Tom pointed out.

'The doors aren't the only way out of Kirrin Cottage!' said George. 'Now, quick! Hurry! And don't forget dog biscuits for Gilbert!'

Ten minutes later, the five of them had reassembled in the study, fully dressed and each carrying a backpack. George's looked the heaviest, with several bulging pockets dotted all over it.

'What are we going to do?' hissed Tom. 'Why don't we just stay here like he told us?'

'And let him get the treasure?' George replied. 'I don't think so!'

'What is this treasure, anyway?' asked Maddy, fascinated.

'I'll tell you the whole story once we're out of here,' promised George. 'Ready for an adventure?'

'No,' blurted Tom immediately.

'Adventures always come to the adventurous,' said George, with a smile and a glance at his sisters. 'Now, stay quiet. You're going to like this.'

Maddy, in spite of her nervousness, grinned back at this mysterious professor. She could feel a tingle of excitement mingled with the salty sea breeze streaming through the open window.

George crept over to a metal control panel that stood on a plinth beside the far wall. It was studded with switches, knobs and dials, and was connected to the thick tangle of wires that led out of the window and into the metal tower in the garden.

'Ready?' asked George. Tom gave a small whimper, but Maddy and Fran both nodded. 'Good,' the professor replied in a whisper. 'Right – Maddy. Get up on that chair and take the picture off the wall.' She pointed to the oil painting that hung above the fireplace.

'Take down . . . the picture?' Maddy asked. 'But why?'

'You never know what secrets are hidden in a shipwreck,' said George mysteriously. 'Quick!'

Thinking to herself that perhaps the professor had gone a little peculiar after living on her own for so long, Maddy dragged a wooden chair over to the fireplace. Standing on it on tiptoe, she was just able to stretch out her arms and grasp the painting by both sides. It lifted cleanly off its hook, revealing eight solid-looking wooden panels behind. Maddy climbed down off the chair and propped the picture up against the bookcases.

'Get off the rug, all of you,' ordered George. 'And be ready!'

'What's going to happen?' asked Fran, dragging Gilbert off the hearth rug by his collar.

'A diversion.' George flicked a switch on the control panel and the dials lit up. 'Followed by an escape.' And she spun the largest dial all the way to the right. Immediately, there was a high-pitched whining sound. Through the window they could see that the wires sticking out of the tower in the garden had begun to glow. There was a shout of alarm from the man by the wall. Then a pop, a flash of light from the tower, and thick white smoke began to stream from the control panel, swirling across the room and quickly hiding the windows.

'That'll keep them busy for a moment,' said George in a satisfied tone. She raced back across the room and rolled back the corner of the hearth rug, revealing more of the stone floor. Then she leapt nimbly up on to the chair and pressed on one of the wooden panels. It slid smoothly sideways, and George reached inside and pulled on a hidden lever.

There was a deep clunk, and one of the stones that made up the floor tilted on its side. All three children gasped in amazement. 'Get your bags!' George told them, sliding the panel back into place and jumping back down from the chair. On one side of the stone were ancient stairs leading down into the darkness.

'What's down there?' said Maddy, torn between anxiety and excitement.

'Our escape route,' George told her. 'Always have an escape plan.'

'I've got a torch!' said Fran, rummaging in her backpack and pulling out a small orange flashlight she'd brought with her.

'That's not a torch,' said George with a smile, reaching into one of the side pockets of her own rucksack.

'*That*'s a torch,' she went on, displaying a large, silver cylinder. She pushed a button, and a bright beam illuminated the stone stairs. 'Quick!' George led the way downwards. Without thinking they followed, Fran giving Gilbert an encouraging pat.

When they reached the bottom of the stone staircase, George pulled on a wire set into the wall, and the entrance behind them swung smoothly and quietly closed on some hidden mechanism. 'And this is a little addition,' she said with a smile, pressing a button. There was a swish and a clunk from somewhere above.

'What was that?' asked Fran.

'Electromagnet,' the professor explained. 'It's pulled the rug back into place, hiding the entrance. Bit of a dead giveaway, otherwise. They'll never work out where we've gone.'

'This is utterly, completely brilliant!' said Maddy, her voice echoing back strangely from the walls of the secret passageway.

'We found this a long, long time ago,' said George over her shoulder, leading them at a fast pace away from Kirrin Cottage. The tunnel was high enough to stand up in, although at times it was so narrow that they had to squeeze sideways. 'I've made a few improvements over the years. Like I said, it's always good to have an escape plan, especially with the work I do. This used to lead to a farmhouse, but we can't go appearing at the back of someone's wardrobe in the middle of the night. Luckily, I added another exit a few years back. Here, this way!'

She flashed her torch on to the left-hand wall, revealing an archway lined with modern-looking metal beams. Another set of newer-looking stairs led upwards. The children followed George up, and she tugged a lever set into the wall. Above them, a hatchway opened, and they climbed out into the fresh air. At least, it was fresher than the air in the tunnel. They were in the corner of a large barn, filled with cows sleeping placidly in stalls.

'Pee-*yew*!' said Tom in a loud whisper. 'It *stinks*!'

'Good clean farmyard smell,' George told him. 'Come on! Don't wake them.' They crept between the cows and out of the barn right at the edge of a large farm. Smart buildings stood nearby, with the words SANDERS' DAIRY painted on the side. Maddy remembered the ice cream they had bought at the beach – it seemed like months ago, but she realised it had only been that morning. So much had happened since then.

George took them out of the farm and along a potholed concrete track that led steeply uphill. To their left they could see Kirrin Cottage in the near distance, with the moonlit sea beyond. After a while, they turned up a narrow footpath towards the trees at the top of the hill. The leaves were giving out a constant, hissing whisper as they blew to and fro, and Fran felt a slight shiver as she looked up at the dark woods. They followed George along the path, which soon reached a wide clearing where logs had been placed around a stone firepit. 'I come out here when I need to get away sometimes,' George told them. 'You lot get some food out while I get a fire going.' She pulled matches from her rucksack and began to gather some of the fallen, dry wood that lay all around.

Twenty minutes later, the three children, George and Gilbert were sitting on the logs, with the golden light of a crackling fire flickering in front of them. They were feeling too full of excitement to sleep.

'So,' said Maddy, munching on a sausage roll. 'Is this the part where you tell us what's going on?'

'I think it is,' replied George. 'I'll answer your questions, then we'll get some sleep. It's going to be a busy day tomorrow.'

'What, sleep *here*?' asked Tom, looking around the clearing, horrified. 'In the open air?'

'It'll be the best night's sleep you've had in ages,' George promised him. 'Now, what do you want to know?'

All through their underground journey Maddy had been trying to put her thoughts in order. And now, she was ready. She ticked the questions off on her fingers as she asked, 'Who is that man? How do you know him? What is the treasure? Where is it hidden? How is he going to get hold of it and' – she glanced around at her brother and sister – 'how are we going to help you get it back?'

Fran and Tom nodded in agreement.

'All excellent questions,' George told her, 'especially that last one. All right then.' She settled herself more comfortably on the log. 'I hope you're ready for a story. Because this happened a long, long time ago . . .'

FIFTY-FIVE
YEARS
EARLIER . . .

6

The Train to Kirrin

George heard the distant shriek of the train's whistle and grinned to herself. 'Not long now, Tim,' she said to the large, shaggy mongrel who sat obediently at her feet on the station platform.

'Wuff,' replied Timmy. He was just as excited as his mistress about seeing her three cousins. The first few weeks of the summer holidays had dragged terribly without their company.

All around them was bustle and busyness as the people at Kirrin station got ready for the train's arrival. A porter in his smart uniform trundled a cart full of suitcases up the platform, and children craned their necks to peer down the line, hoping to be the first to catch a glimpse of the engine. 'There it is!' cried a little girl in pigtails, as a bright green steam train appeared from a cutting and made its way down the shallow slope into the station.

Timmy got to his feet and capered around, as George scanned the faces peeking out of the open windows. Before long she caught sight of the bright blonde hair of her cousin Anne, who waved frantically.

'George!' Anne cried. 'Hallo, hallo! Julian, Dick!' she called back over her shoulder into the carriage. 'We're here! I can see the sea! Oh, did you ever in your life see anything so blue?'

As soon as the train juddered to a halt, Anne opened the door and leapt out. George and Timmy raced down the platform towards her. 'Timmy!' she squealed, burying her face in the big dog's thick coat. 'Did you miss us, boy? Did you?'

'Any chance of some help here?' came a voice from behind her as her brothers, Julian and Dick, struggled with the suitcases. Anne gasped.

'Sorry, Ju!' she exclaimed. 'I was just so excited to be back at Kirrin again!'

'I'll help,' said George, leaping up into the carriage and grabbing two of the bags from Dick. Before long all four children, with the dog scampering around them, were heading out of the station and along the road towards Kirrin Village.

'There's so much to do, I don't know where to begin,' said Dick, his eyes shining with excitement. 'A bathe in the sea, a visit to the island . . . but let's start with tea at Kirrin Cottage! I wonder if Joanna's made one of her wonderful sponge cakes!'

'She has,' confirmed George, her own grin matching her cousin's. Her heart swelled with happiness. For many years she had been a rather lonely and solitary girl, until Julian, Dick and Anne had come to stay. Now the four of them – along with Timmy of course – were firm friends. And they had been on many exciting adventures too!

'You'll never guess what?' George told the others as they walked through the small seaside village. Fishing boats were pulled up next to the wooden dock, with seagulls wheeling overhead. 'Father says we can go camping on Kirrin Island again for a few days!'

'Oh, Kirrin Island,' said Anne, squinting across the dazzling water to peer at the rocky island with its ruined castle, far out in the bay. 'How super! I wonder if the rabbits are as tame as ever!'

'Woof!' said Timmy. He loved visiting Kirrin Island as much as the rest of them, mainly because he usually got to share in whatever delicious picnic food the children brought with them. But he simply couldn't understand why he wasn't allowed to chase the rabbits who hopped here and there among the gorse bushes. He was a dog! Chasing rabbits was his job!

'No, Tim,' said Dick seriously. 'I know exactly what you're barking, and it's not allowed. Do you know, I really think I can understand what old Tim's saying? I should take an exam in dog language instead of French next term!' Julian gave him a grin and a friendly shove as they left the seafront and began to climb the hill towards Kirrin Cottage.

'What have you been up to for the last two weeks, George?' asked Anne. 'You can't have been bored *all* the time?'

'Well,' said George, pulling a large, folded piece of paper out of her pocket. 'I kept myself busy some of the time working on this.' Her cousins clustered around her on the road as she unfolded it to reveal a map.

'It's Kirrin Bay!' exclaimed Julian. 'Look' – he pointed – 'there's the island! And what are these markings around it?'

'I've been plotting the positions of some of the rocks,' George explained, 'I've been out in the boat measuring where they are. I thought, as it's *my* island, I should have a record of the waters all around it.' Kirrin Island did indeed belong to George – and it was surrounded by dangerous rocks which made it impossible for most boats to land there.

'You wouldn't want anyone else getting hold of that map then!' said Dick with a laugh. 'If everyone knew the way through the rocks, your island would soon be full of daytrippers and their picnics!'

George scowled. She simply couldn't stand the idea of strangers on Kirrin Island. Quickly she folded the map up and put it back in her pocket. 'I won't *ever* let anybody get hold of it,' she promised. 'My sea chart is a secret!'

'Here we are,' announced Julian presently. 'Kirrin Cottage at last!' The large white house, hundreds of years old, stood right at the edge of the town, with the green of the moor rising behind it, dotted with smudges of yellow gorse flowers.

George's mother was kneeling beside the vegetable patch in the garden, a straw bonnet on her head and a basket beside her. 'Hallo!' she called, waving. 'Goodness, it's so nice to see you all! George has missed you terribly. She's so longed for you five to be together again!'

'Hallo, Aunt Fanny,' said Julian, opening the gate and leading the way across the garden. 'Thanks awfully for having us! It really wouldn't seem like the summer hols without a visit to Kirrin.'

'And an adventure!' added Dick.

'No adventures this time,' insisted Anne. 'Just for once, I want to bathe in the sea and picnic on the sand with sandwiches and cold ginger beer and read my new book. We've had enough adventures to last us a lifetime already!'

'There's always room for one more,' Dick told her, peering into his aunt's basket. 'I say, what's this? Radishes? My favourite! Is it nearly lunchtime, Aunt Fanny?'

His aunt laughed. 'Some things never change, at least! Yes, the bell for lunch should be going any minute now. But we might need to wait for your father, George. He had some last-minute visitors that I wasn't expecting.'

'Visitors?' echoed George with a frown. 'What visitors? Not more scientists!' George's father, Uncle Quentin, was a famous scientist, and often received visits from other men and women who were researching the same areas as him. They were often bad-tempered, just like he was, and very likely to object to the noises made by four excitable children, not to mention a high-spirited dog.

'No, not scientists,' Aunt Fanny told her. 'At least, not the same kind as your father. She's a very famous archaeologist who's working on a dig up at Whispering Wood. I'm not sure what they've discovered up there, but it's been going on for a few weeks now. She's here with her son and I've no idea what they want with your father.'

Just then, the back door opened, to reveal Joanna, the cook. 'There you are at last!' she said, beaming all over her kindly face.

'Hallo, dear Joanna,' said Dick. 'Yes, here we all are! Hungry as hunters and ready to do full justice to one of your famous lunches!' Joanna laughed. She loved nothing more than having her cooking appreciated – and nobody appreciated it more than Dick!

'I was just about to ring the bell,' she told them. 'So hurry upstairs and wash your hands.' The children piled into Kirrin Cottage in a flurry of excitement, their aunt following them with her basket over her arm. But before they could carry their suitcases up to their usual bedrooms, there was the sound of a door opening and the stern voice of George's father echoed through the house.

'Fanny! Fanny, where are you? I have some very important news!'

'Following everything so far?' asked George, fifty-five years later.

'I have so *many* questions already,' said Maddy. The three children were sitting on the soft carpet of leaves, their backs against one of the tree trunks that still felt warm from the day's sunshine. Although the sky was pitch black, the embers of George's campfire cast a comforting light that was a barrier against the rustling leaves and night time noises of the woods all around them.

'Questions? Already?' said George, getting up and throwing another log on to the fire. 'But I haven't even got to the mystery yet. What questions can you possibly have?'

'Well, firstly,' said Tom, 'did you really used to talk like that?'

'Like what?' The dim firelight showed a puzzled frown on George's face.

'You know – "super", "summer hols", "Gosh, Aunt Fanny, you are a brick."'

'Well, for a start,' George replied, sitting back down opposite, 'nobody's called anybody a brick as far as I recall. But yes, people talked a bit differently back then. A lot of things have moved on.'

'Well, you certainly used to eat differently!' blurted Maddy. 'Radishes? And ginger beer? Gross!'

'And,' Fran had been bursting to say this, 'you used to have a dog! I knew you did! Why were you so mean to Gilbert when we arrived?' Gilbert, who was curled up by her side, twitched in his sleep.

George looked slightly awkward but didn't directly answer that question. 'Look,' she said, 'if you keep butting in like this, we'll be here all night. And we'll need to get some sleep if we're going to save the treasure. Why don't you let me finish the story, and then you can ask me whatever you like tomorrow?'

'OK,' agreed Maddy reluctantly.

'I still can't believe it,' said Tom. 'Grandad seriously used to get that enthusiastic about radishes? But yes, you can finish the story.'

'Thank you,' said George sarcastically. 'Ah, yes. So, my cousins had just arrived at Kirrin when my father *called us all into his study. This was not going to be the relaxing summer break that your Great-aunt Anne was hoping for! Things were about to get very mysterious indeed . . .'*

7

A Stranger – and a Shock!

The Five followed Aunt Fanny into Uncle Quentin's study. It was a large room with windows overlooking the garden – and it was usually completely off-limits as he worked on his latest experiments. Inside, the children couldn't help looking at the wooden panels above the fireplace. One exciting Christmas they had discovered an old piece of paper that revealed one of them was the key to opening what the centuries-old writing called a *via occulta* – a secret passageway that led from this very room! But today the hearth rug lay over the stone that was the entrance to the passageway.

Uncle Quentin, his thick brows as forbidding as ever, looked at them sharply as they approached. 'Ah, Georgina,' he said in a satisfied tone, 'your cousins have arrived, good. What I have to say concerns all of you.'

George scowled. She absolutely hated being called by her full name, and usually refused to answer. Even the teachers at the school she attended alongside Anne had quickly taken to calling her George.

'Good afternoon, sir,' said Julian politely to his uncle, who gave a grunt of approval. He wasn't generally that comfortable in the company of children, who often let off loud noises without any warning or made jokes his scientific brain couldn't understand. But he didn't mind tall, clear-eyed Julian, who seemed so much older than his age.

A woman sat next to Uncle Quentin in a comfortable leather armchair, smiling at them broadly. She had a friendly, open face and was wearing stout boots with khaki trousers tucked into them. She looked as if she lived the kind of outdoorsy life that they all enjoyed the most. 'Hallo there!' she cried. 'Why, I've just been hearing what wonderful children you all are, and now I see you I realise straight away that it must be true!'

All the children greeted her, apart from George who was still smarting from her father's use of her name and only managed a rather curt nod.

'This is Mrs Humphries,' explained Uncle Quentin. 'The celebrated archaeologist.'

'Now, really,' said Mrs Humphries modestly. 'Quentin! You'll be giving me a swollen head. But it's true,' she told the children. 'Not sure about "celebrated", but I certainly am an archaeologist. I'm excavating some of the old burial mounds up in the woods there.' She pointed out of the window towards the distant trees on the clifftop.

'Mrs Humphries has come to ask if her son can stay with us for a few days,' said Uncle Quentin.

'I've reached a very crucial point in the dig, you see,' she explained, 'and I really don't have time to look after poor Raymond.' She pointed to a spot behind the cousins, and they turned with surprise to see a boy standing quietly in the corner, almost hidden by the open door. He was short, with untidy brown hair, and he looked sad and sulky.

'I've told Mrs Humphries that we'll be delighted to have Raymond to stay,' announced Uncle Quentin. 'He can go camping on the island with you other children. It'll be a nice little holiday for him while his mother completes her important work.'

Julian, Dick and Anne stood in silence, but not George. She had spent the last fortnight longing for her cousins to arrive. And now her father was saddling them with this miserable-looking little boy. It was unthinkable. She stamped her foot in rage.

'I *won't* have this boy to stay on my island!' she told her father furiously. 'How dare you suggest it! I simply *won't*!' And she stormed out of the room.

'I must apologise for my daughter,' said Uncle Quentin, suddenly looking exactly like George as he gave a furious scowl.

'Of course your son can stay with us.' Aunt Fanny jumped in, smoothing over the awkward situation as usual. It wasn't the first time her hot-headed husband had fallen out with their equally hot-headed daughter. 'Hallo, Raymond,' she said to the boy, beckoning him forward into the room. 'Why don't you come and meet the others? Please don't worry about George, she will soon calm down.'

'Yes, hallo,' said Julian, holding out his hand. 'I'm Julian. This is my brother Dick, and our little sister Anne. Pleased to meet you.' The boy gave Julian's hand a very limp shake.

'Lovely,' said Mrs Humphries, clapping her hands. 'I can already tell that you children are going to be very great friends! Isn't that right, Raymond?'

'Yes, Mother,' the boy replied in a meek, unhappy voice. Anne frowned and looked sharply at Mrs Humphries as if she sensed something strange, but Dick was already moving forward to shake his hand and welcome him to Kirrin Cottage. He received nothing in reply but a quiet grunt and an expression of pure misery.

Lunch that day was not the joyful occasion the children had been expecting. They had hoped to be celebrating being Five again, but Aunt Fanny had ordered George to her bedroom as a punishment for her rude behaviour. Instead, Raymond joined them at the table, still looking pale and thoroughly unhappy. Mrs Humphries, after a private discussion with Aunt Fanny and Uncle Quentin about paying for his board and lodging, had walked away up the hill towards the woods to continue with her archaeology.

'I say,' said Dick excitedly, 'your mother's work does sound awfully fascinating! I love stories about ancient things being dug up. Do you think she's going to find something incredibly important or valuable and be in all the newspapers?'

'I don't know,' Raymond replied, picking at his salad and refusing to meet Dick's eye.

Julian also decided to engage this odd, quiet boy in conversation. 'Well,' he said, 'do you think we might be able to go and have a look around her dig one day? I agree with Dick, it does sound very interesting.'

'I don't think so, no,' said Raymond. And after that, Julian and Dick gave up on trying to draw him out. They began to entertain the rest of the table with stories about what had happened at school the previous term. Raymond finished his meal in silence. Only Anne, who felt sorry for the boy, managed to catch his eye once, and gave him a friendly smile. He gave a small smile back before the strange, frightened expression flitted across his face once again. Anne frowned. Something definitely wasn't right here!

8

On Kirrin Island Again

'Well,' said Dick to Julian the following morning, 'I can't see that young Ray is going to be much fun to spend time with.' The two boys had left Raymond sleeping and crept downstairs to the garden.

'No,' said Julian, frowning. The previous afternoon the two boys had done their best to cheer Raymond up, taking him down to the beach in the afternoon and asking him to play cards with them in the evening after tea. But the boy had kept his miserable expression in place all day. The only person he had really spoken to was Anne, who had done her best to be kind to him.

George, when she had been allowed to join them after lunch, had simply spent most of the day pretending he wasn't there.

'Ray of sunshine, that's what I'll call him!' said Dick, laughing. 'Our own little Ray of sunshine!'

'I just hope he won't spoil the hols completely,' said Julian seriously. 'I know George is furious that he's coming to the island with us today.' The children were due to set off for Kirrin Island in George's boat that very afternoon – and Uncle Quentin was insisting that they take Raymond along. 'Perhaps some fresh sea air and exercise will cheer him up a bit.'

'Or maybe Mrs Humphries will finish her digging and take him off our hands,' countered Dick. 'That's what I'd like the most! Although I'm determined to go and visit her at work some time this week. It really does sound fascinating!'

'Yes, we'll definitely do that, whether Raymond wants us to or not,' said Julian. He was also itching to visit a real team of archaeologists who might be discovering ancient treasure. 'A visit to his mother,' he reasoned, 'will probably cheer him up a bit!' Dick shrugged uncertainly.

The rest of the morning was spent in a flurry of packing. Blankets, rugs and cushions all had to be carried down to George's boat, followed by several baskets of delicious food that Joanna had been busily preparing. Finally, with the summer sun beating down on the sea, it was time to set off. Raymond followed the four children and Timmy down the hill to the beach, dragging his feet in the dust and still looking as glum as anything.

'Come on, Ray of sunshine!' called Dick, making George laugh. 'Kirrin Island really is a marvellous place! It might even be enough to put a smile on *your* face!'

'Leave him alone,' scolded Anne. 'You're not going to make him any happier by teasing him!' Ray gave her another of his thin, watery smiles.

George held the boat steady while the others took off their sandals and waded into the warm, shallow water to climb in. It really did feel wonderful to have the sand between their toes and see Kirrin Island

waiting for them in the distance. Timmy paddled gleefully over and shook himself dry once Julian had helped him on board. 'Hey!' protested Dick as seawater and sand flew from his coat. 'Careful, Tim! You're creating a sandstorm.' The others laughed, apart from Raymond, who was sitting quietly on the folded blankets, gazing with sad eyes up at the woods on top of the cliffs.

It was a hot afternoon, but there was a pleasant breeze blowing out to sea. Before long, the sail of George's boat was puffed out proudly, and the water under the prow was making a wonderful bubbling noise as she sailed them deftly out into the bay. Kirrin was soon a toy town behind them.

All around the little boat, there were white caps in the otherwise calm water, revealing the location of the many hidden rocks that protected Kirrin Island. Here and there, spiky grey patches of them were visible, sticking out of the sea. It was an extremely dangerous place to sail if you didn't know the secret route through the rocks. Any boat coming close to Kirrin Island that wasn't aware of this route was sure to get shipwrecked. But George had been sailing these waters ever since she was tiny. 'Ready about!' she warned as she prepared to turn towards the island.

'That means you need to duck,' Anne warned Raymond kindly. 'The boom – that bit of wood at the bottom of the sail – is going to come swinging across, and you don't want a bump on the head.' The boy dutifully bent over as the sail pivoted to the other side and the sound of the water changed as George steered them expertly towards her secret, sheltered cove. Very soon she was pulling down the sail as the boat drifted into a calm bay with tall rock faces on either side. Julian readily leapt out and pulled it firmly up on to the sand.

'It really feels like coming home, doesn't it?' said Anne delightedly, looking around her. There was no sound except the gentle lapping waves and the '*chack, chack, chack*' of the jackdaws who nested in the highest tower of the ruined castle.

'Shall we have lunch straight away?' asked Dick hopefully. 'I'm starving!'

'You're always hungry!' Julian laughed. 'Yes, all right. How about it, Anne? Picnic lunch in the castle courtyard?'

'Very well then,' said Anne, smiling. 'Bring up the baskets and a couple of rugs.'

Twenty minutes later, they were all contentedly munching among the ruined walls of Kirrin Castle. It had been abandoned hundreds of years before and spiky sea grass and patches of gorse now grew among the tumbled stones. Rabbits hopped here and there, completely comfortable with the presence of the children. Timmy gave a small whine, but George placed a hand on his collar and he reluctantly sat down.

'Ginger beer or lemonade?' asked Anne, opening a large basket.

'Ginger beer, please!' Dick replied, lying back and looking up at the blue sky as he took a large bite out of his sandwich. 'I can't imagine why all meals aren't eaten like this. There's something about fresh air and sunshine that makes everything taste better. I swear this egg and tomato sandwich wouldn't be half as good eaten indoors!'

'Do you know, I think you're right,' agreed Julian, who was propped up against a sun-warmed stone nearby. 'Pass me one of those hard-boiled eggs, would you, Anne? If Dick hasn't scoffed them all already, that is!'

'Here you are,' said Anne, getting up and brushing the sand from her skirt. 'And, look, I brought a little pot of salt. Boiled eggs aren't the same without salt.'

'Whatever would we do without you, little Anne?' said Julian, grinning. 'You really are wonderful.'

'And not just because I supply you with food, I hope?' asked Anne. 'What about you, Raymond? What else would you like to eat?' Just as on the boat journey, Raymond was sitting a little way apart from the other children. He had nibbled on a sandwich but hardly spoken, only mumbling, 'Thanks,' when Anne handed it to him.

'Yes, come on, Ray,' said Dick. 'Do cheer up! You're here on a real-life island – and I promise you, we're very nice people! There's no need to look so miserable all the time.' But the boy didn't even seem to hear him. Timmy got up and plonked himself down in the warm sand beside him, but Raymond even ignored the big dog. George looked across and screwed up her mouth crossly. If this boy couldn't even be nice to Timmy, then she certainly couldn't be bothered with him!

After lunch, it was too hot to do anything except lie around in the sandy courtyard. Rabbits hopped to and fro, jackdaws wheeled overhead and the tower cast a long, cool shadow. Before long, all five children and Timmy had fallen fast asleep.

9

Strange Lights in the Night

Timmy was the first to wake. The large brown dog twitched an ear and opened an eye to see a rabbit, not three paces away, looking at him keenly with its bright little eyes. It had hopped closer to get a better look at this strange visitor. Timmy let out a startled 'Wuff!' and the rabbit fled.

'What is it, Tim?' asked Dick, rolling over and rubbing his eyes. 'I say, what time is it? I feel as if I've slept for days.'

Julian checked his watch. 'Almost five o'clock.'

'Goodness,' said Anne. 'And we haven't even started

to unpack yet! We had better get everything ready before it starts to get dark! We'll need to cut heather for our beds and unload the boat. There's so much to do!'

'All right, all right,' agreed Julian, getting to his feet and stretching. 'Dick and I will get everything from the boat. Where shall we sleep? In the cave?'

'Oh, no!' said George, also getting up. 'It's far too nice to be down in the cave. I want to sleep under the stars!' On a previous visit to the island, the Five had discovered a hidden cave in the cliffs on one side of the island. It was wonderful and cool with a sandy floor, and they reached it through a small hole in the roof – or by a dangerous scramble across the rocks on the shore.

'George is right,' decided Julian. 'We'll make our beds in the castle. It'll be wonderful to wake up here.'

'But we'll use the cave as a larder,' decided Anne. 'The food will stay fresher down there, where it's cool.'

The next two hours went by in a flurry of activity. Julian and Dick went back down to the boat, and after making sure it was tied up securely, they carried the bags and baskets up the shallow slope into the castle. George, with some reluctant help from the still-silent Raymond, went to fetch armfuls of heather, which Anne made into five snug beds, covering them with blankets and tucking in the corners neatly. 'There!' she said. 'You won't find a more comfortable bed anywhere in the whole country – if not the world! Now, Julian, will you please light a fire? I think we're all ready for a cup of tea.'

Before long the kettle was singing merrily among the embers and supper was made. As the shadows of twilight began to collect among the tumbled walls of Kirrin Castle, Dick raised his hands to the darkening sky and let out an enormous yawn.

'Now you've set me off!' said George, yawning widely herself. 'Don't you know that they're catching?' And before long, nobody could help themselves. All the children were yawning – even Timmy joined in.

'I vote we clean our teeth and get to bed,' said Julian. 'I'm not sure I can keep awake much longer anyway! Then we can wake up with the sun and bathe before breakfast.' Everyone agreed this sounded like a splendid plan – the sea would be so cool and refreshing before the heat of the day began to build.

Soon, there was no sound in the warm evening except their soft breathing. Timmy, curled up at George's feet as usual, took one last look around. Good – all five children seemed to be fast asleep. His job protecting them was done for the day. It was just such a shame he hadn't been allowed to chase that rabbit! With a sigh, he placed his shaggy head on his front paws and, within minutes, he was fast asleep himself.

But Timmy had been wrong. Not all the children were asleep. Julian and Dick certainly were. Unhappy-looking Raymond Humphries was. But George lay wide awake with her brain buzzing.

She had spent the last two weeks counting the hours until her cousins would come to visit, keeping herself busy in her boat by carefully rowing around the island and plotting the rocks on her sea chart, but she couldn't wait to be Five again. And now Raymond had arrived and spoilt it all. George looked over at the sleeping boy and gave a sharp sigh. Then she threw off her blanket and climbed the low hill on one side of the castle, picking her way between the large gorse bushes. Perhaps the night air blowing in from the sea would make her sleepy.

George stood on the hill and looked back across the midnight bay towards the coast. There was Kirrin itself, with a few lights still burning in the windows. She looked to the left, and felt sure that one of the golden, twinkling lights higher up the hill must be the windows of Kirrin Cottage itself. Perhaps her father was up late working – it wasn't unusual for him to stay up all night when he was trying to solve some troublesome problem or design an experiment.

'George,' came a low whisper from behind her. There was a crackling from the gorse, and Anne appeared. 'Can't you sleep either?' she asked.

'No,' George told her.

'Are you worried about Raymond too?' asked her cousin, reaching the top of the hill.

'Worried about him?' scoffed George angrily.

'What's there to be worried about? He's ruining our holiday! I wish he—' But suddenly she broke off. 'What is *that*?' she asked, pointing inland.

'What? Where?' asked Anne, straining her eyes to follow George's pointing finger. She stared up towards the cliffs to the left of Kirrin Village. Right on the top, the trees of Whispering Wood stood out dark against the sky.

'Look,' said George, 'near the cliff edge. A light!'

Anne gave a small gasp of shock. Sure enough, there among the trees was a strange red light. It shone brightly in the forest like some sinister eye, disappearing now and then as the branches waved in the wind.

'Whatever is it?' asked George. 'No, wait. There are two of them!' Away to the right was another light – this time a faint greenish colour and higher up.

'Do you think it's something to do with the archaeologists?' Anne wondered out loud.

'Why would they be digging in the dark?' countered George. 'And why use coloured lanterns?'

The pair watched the lights for a while, glittering strangely up in the dark forest. But before long the sea air did its work and they finally began to feel sleepy. They picked their way back down the hill and fell into their heather beds. Anne was asleep almost before her head hit the rolled-up coat she was using as a pillow. But George lay awake for a few minutes more, feeling determined to visit Raymond's mother and investigate those strange lights.

As planned, the children bathed the following morning and as expected, the sea was wonderfully refreshing. Around the island shore was a perfect pool with a deep, sandy floor, protected from the waves by a high wall of rocks. Crabs scuttled for cover far below them as Julian, Dick, Anne and George splashed, dived and ducked. Raymond sat quietly on his towel nearby, having told the others glumly that he 'didn't swim very well'.

'What a surprise,' said Dick, throwing up his hands in mock despair before challenging Julian to a swimming race.

It was only when they were lolling on the sand waiting for the early sun to dry them off that Anne remembered her strange experience the previous night. 'Raymond,' she asked, 'do you know why there would be coloured lights up in the woods at night? Is it anything to do with your mother's work?'

'Coloured lights?' asked Dick, intrigued. Anne told the others about what she had seen.

'You were half-asleep,' Dick pointed out. 'What if you just dreamt it?'

'She didn't!' broke in George hotly. 'I was there too, and there were definitely lights in the woods!

'You might have seen a star through the trees,' said Julian. 'Yes, I bet that's it! Mars looks a bit red sometimes, and the stars were very bright last night.'

'I think we should ask Mrs Humphries,' said George, not convinced. Mars might be red, but whoever heard of a green star?

'Well,' mused Julian. 'I'm certainly desperate to go and see a real archaeological dig.'

'Yes,' agreed Dick, 'how about it, Ray of sunshine? Shall we pay your mother a visit? That might put a smile on your face.'

But far from putting a smile on his face, the prospect of visiting the archaeological site at Whispering Wood seemed to horrify Raymond. His face turned even paler than usual, and his mouth drooped. 'No, no,' he muttered. 'I think . . . I think she's too busy.'

'Nonsense,' decided Julian. 'Dick's right – perhaps it will help to cheer you up a bit. It's decided – we'll go tomorrow! We'll need to go ashore anyway to pick up some fresh supplies.' And, very reluctantly, Raymond nodded.

'He doesn't seem very excited about seeing his mother, does he?' asked Julian quietly later. He and Anne were tending to the campfire while the others dozed. 'I wonder why.'

'There's something very strange going on,' agreed Anne. 'It's a mystery.'

'I wonder if we're about to find ourselves in the middle of another adventure,' whispered Julian excitedly, placing another dry log on the fire.

'I was looking forward to a peaceful couple of weeks,' said Anne with a sigh. 'But adventures always find us, whether we're looking for them or not!'

10

The Burial Barrows

As the children approached Whispering Wood the following afternoon, it was clear where its name had come from. The large woodland stood right on top of the cliffs on a high hill overlooking Kirrin Bay. Up here, the wind made the leaves give a constant, rustling sigh and it was easy to believe that the trees really were whispering to each other. Anne hurried to catch up with Julian, Dick, George and Timmy.

'Where is this dig, then?' asked Julian. 'Raymond?' Raymond was lagging far behind.

'I know where it is,' said George confidently. 'Never mind him.' She had been coming to these old woods behind her house to play ever since she was small. 'The old burial mounds are over there' – she pointed – 'in a hidden glade right at the top of the hill. Come on.' She led them through the trees, picking up paths here and there but mostly finding her way through memory, just as she did through the rocks that lay around Kirrin Island. Timmy darted ahead, clearly knowing his way through the wood just as well as his mistress.

They climbed upwards constantly, surrounded at all times by the murmuring and hissing of the leaves overhead. Eventually the trees cleared and they found themselves on the lip of a large, circular clearing right at the top of the forest. It was surrounded by what had once been a wall, though grass had long since grown over it. In the centre of the clearing were three high, conical heaps: the ancient burial mounds. George had scaled them many times before to enjoy the fine sea views from the top. But today things looked very different.

Instead of the usual peaceful clearing at the top of

the forest, the Five looked out across a busy archaeological dig. Planks led up the side of the central burial mound, and a deep, muddy trench had been dug right across the top. A man in filthy work clothes was trudging towards a row of big, pointed tents that had been set up on the other side of the clearing.

'Those mounds are called barrows,' said Dick. 'We learnt about these in school. Long ago, important people would be buried beneath them – along with all their treasure! Ancient people believed they would take it with them to the afterlife.'

'Treasure!' breathed Julian excitedly. 'Just imagine!'

Just then, the children caught sight of Mrs Humphries. She was standing right at the top of the central barrow, talking to another man. When she saw the children, a strange expression crossed her face. She was too far away to tell for sure, but George felt certain that instead of being pleased to see them, she looked disbelieving and furious. Her cheeks coloured with an angry red flush, and she spoke more urgently to the man, who quickly hurried away towards the line of tents. Mrs Humphries began to make her way down the planks towards them.

'She doesn't seem terribly glad we're visiting,' said George uncertainly.

'Did you notice that?' said Anne. 'I thought she seemed awfully angry.'

'Nonsense,' said Julian easily. 'I'm sure she's just busy. After all, she said we could come and visit. Don't worry, little Anne. Let me handle it.' Now it was Anne's turn to flush an angry red. She might be the youngest, but she was growing tired of nobody paying her opinions any attention.

'Hallo there, all of you,' called Mrs Humphries, marching towards them. She was holding a trowel in one hand and had a straw hat tied firmly on her head with a white scarf. 'I wasn't expecting to see you so soon. Hallo, Raymond dear! Are you having a nice time with your new friends? All calm and quiet?' The four other children turned to look at Raymond and were startled to see that he was looking at Mrs Humphries with an expression of open dislike, if not actual hatred.

'I said,' repeated Mrs Humphries, reaching them and putting her arm around Raymond, 'is everything calm? Honestly, darling! Do answer, or these nice children will think there's something frightfully strange going on!' George, who was closest, saw the knuckles of her hand whiten as she squeezed his shoulder.

'Yes, Mother,' said Raymond in a flat voice. 'All is calm. Sorry, Mother.'

'That's better,' said Mrs Humphries briskly. 'Now, I expect you've come to see the dig! There isn't much time to show you around, I'm afraid, because we're very busy. But I can spare you five minutes. Come along. This way!'

The children had hoped to get a proper look at how a real-life archaeologist worked, but they were soon sadly disappointed. Mrs Humphries led them straight to the trench in the main burial mound, warning them curtly, 'You can't go inside. Much too dangerous.' They peered into the deep trench, which cut right through the centre of the barrow. On either side, stone openings led into darkness. How they longed to explore them!

'Is that where the treasure would have been buried?' asked Dick, his eyes shining.

Mrs Humphries rounded on him. 'Treasure?' she said sharply. 'What do you mean?'

Dick took a step backwards, startled by this response, and Julian had to grab his arm to stop him falling off the narrow planks. 'My brother learnt at school about the treasure people used to bury in barrows like this,' he explained, confused.

'Oh!' Mrs Humphries took a deep breath in and seemed to collect herself. 'I see. No, no,' she went on airily. 'There's no such thing here. We need to be very careful about rumours like that getting around. Don't we, Raymond dear?' She gave a stern look at Raymond, who seemed to writhe away from her. 'Follow me, all of you,' said Mrs Humphries abruptly, striding away from them towards the tents. She disappeared through the flaps of the first one, and they filed in after her. There, laid out on a trestle table, were a few pieces of broken pottery. They looked muddy, brown and deeply uninteresting.

'That's the only "treasure" we're finding here,' Mrs Humphries told them. 'Of course, to an archaeologist like me it's fascinating. But there's no buried gold.

Anything of that kind was taken by grave robbers long, long ago. This isn't some adventure story, you know!' She gave a tinkling little laugh.

The mention of adventure jogged George's memory. 'Why are there coloured lights in the trees?' she asked.

Mrs Humphries, who was bent over the table examining the dirty shards of pottery, froze. 'Lights?' she asked in a clipped tone. 'Whatever can you mean?'

'We saw them last night from the island,' Anne broke in. And now Mrs Humphries stood upright and turned towards them with the most peculiar expression on her face. She was still smiling, but her eyes were narrowed with steely dislike.

'What . . . very observant children you are,' she said. 'Raymond, I do hope you'll keep your new friends out of trouble. Curiosity can be most . . . dangerous. Don't you agree? And now,' she looked at her watch, 'I really must say goodbye. Lots to do. Off you go, all of you. Quick!' And she marched to the tent doorway and held open the flap for them.

'Well, thanks for showing us around,' said Julian politely. The others followed, all feeling rather confused. This visit hadn't been at all what they'd been expecting.

As they were ushered out of the tent, Timmy stopped completely still and looked towards the other tents away to their left, raising his front paw and uttering a low growl.

'Keep that dog under control,' snapped Mrs Humphries from behind them. 'It's not safe for him to be around the dig. He might get badly hurt. Goodbye!' And with this rather sinister warning, she stalked away from them.

The Five, with Raymond trailing after them, walked off down the forest path.

'Well,' said George after a while, 'that was all rather peculiar.'

'It was, a bit,' agreed Julian. 'But I suppose, as Mrs Humphries says, real archaeology isn't quite like the stories. They're not really digging up ancient gold, just some old pots.'

'What a shame,' added Dick. 'Still, Raymond. It

 107

must have been nice for you to visit your mother. Do you feel any more cheerful?'

And it was at this point that something extremely surprising happened. Anne faced the others, so angry that she actually stamped her foot on the forest floor. 'Oh, *honestly!*' she told the rest of the Five furiously. 'Haven't you worked it out?'

'What is the matter, Anne?' asked Julian in astonishment.

'Don't you understand why Raymond's been behaving this way?' Anne went on. 'We're right in the middle of an adventure – and you haven't even realised!'

'Anne's right,' said George. 'We've seen secret lights in the night already and it's clear that not everything on that dig is what it seems to be.'

'It's true things did seem a bit odd there,' agreed Julian. 'But, Anne – what's Raymond got to do with it all?'

'Yes, he just seems miserable all the time,' added Dick. 'Not mysterious!'

'You might be good at solving mysteries about hidden passages,' Anne told her brothers, 'but you've got a lot to learn about *people*! Raymond's not miserable, he's *terrified*.'

They all turned to look at the boy, who was staring at them open-mouthed.

'And what's more,' Anne went on, 'that woman who calls herself Mrs Humphries . . .'

'What about her?' asked Julian, mystified.

'*That's not his mother!*' Anne declared.

11

The Secret of Whispering Wood

George led the children and Timmy to a clearing a little way off the footpath, where stout fallen tree trunks had been arranged in a circle.

As soon as Anne had made her announcement, Raymond had begun to cry bitterly. 'You mustn't say that,' he had sobbed, 'you mustn't!'

'I know you're frightened,' Anne told him. 'But you're going to have to tell us everything.'

George came over to join her. 'She's right. We'll be able to help you, I promise,' she told Raymond kindly.

'And, look here,' added Julian, 'I think Dick and I

owe you an apology. We should have realised that something was badly wrong. I promise you we'll be able to help. But you're going to have to tell the truth. Deal?' Raymond, looking around at the five of them, seemed to consider for a moment and finally gave a small nod. 'Good show,' Julian told him. 'Now, let's sit down and you can tell us the whole tale.'

They took their seats on the logs around the clearing. Raymond blew his nose noisily on a handkerchief Julian handed him before letting out a deep, shuddering sigh and beginning to speak.

'You're right, of course,' he told the Five. 'That woman isn't my mother.' Julian looked across at Anne and gave her a warm smile. She had unlocked the whole mystery. 'My real mother,' Raymond went on, 'is the actual archaeologist in charge of that dig – Hannah Humphries.'

'Then who is *that* imposter?' asked Dick, pointing back up the hill towards the clearing where the burial barrows stood.

'Her name's Sarah Trevelyan,' said Raymond with another sniff. 'She's my mother's assistant. But soon after we began the dig, something incredible happened.

You know all that stuff she was telling you about the grave robbers? That there's nothing really left inside the barrows?'

'Yes,' said Julian, Dick, Anne and George all at once, feeling the familiar prickle of adventure run up their spines.

'Well, that was nonsense,' said Raymond. 'The Whispering Wood barrows were completely untouched and when my mother started digging she found the main burial chamber . . . and the treasure.'

'I KNEW it!' said Dick, getting up and capering around the clearing. 'I *knew* there was treasure! I could feel it in my bones!' Timmy gave a delighted 'Wuff!' of agreement.

'Shh!' Julian told him. 'Don't let them hear! Finish the story, Raymond. I supposed they threatened you, did they?'

'They kidnapped my mother,' Raymond told them. 'Sarah Trevelyan and two men who were here to help with the dig – Spike and Fred. Once they knew there was treasure, they took her prisoner. They're stealing all the gold for themselves.'

'But why send you to Kirrin Cottage?' asked George. 'Why didn't they just keep you captive as well?'

'I was supposed to keep an ear open and warn her if anybody in the village started asking questions,' said Raymond, looking shamefaced. 'That's why she asked me whether things were "all calm" when we went to visit.'

'And you never tried to stand up to them, or fetch help?' asked George heatedly.

'They said they'd hurt my mother if I tried.' Raymond's lip began to quiver.

'Chin up,' Julian told him. 'I know you've been terribly scared, but you don't need to worry any more.' He felt sorry for Raymond, who clearly wasn't very brave. But there was nothing to be done about that right now. They needed a new plan. 'George, you know your way around these woods, don't you?' he asked.

'I've been coming here since before I could walk,' George told him. 'I know every single pathway like the back of my hand.'

'Right,' decided Julian. 'In that case, let's wait for a bit so they think we've sailed away to Kirrin Island.

Then we'll circle round to the back of their camp and see what's going on.'

As they waited in the clearing, the shadows of the trees around them were already beginning to lengthen. Anne dug around in her rucksack and handed round a slab of chocolate, and after another hour had passed, Julian stood up. 'Right then,' he told the others. 'Come on. Let's put a stop to this imposter's plan!'

George kept a warning hand on Timmy's collar as they made their way through the trees, keeping the top of the hill on their left. She didn't want him barking and giving them away. At last, they found themselves back near the cliffs, but on the opposite side of the hill to Kirrin Bay. Here, the woods sloped downhill and then stopped abruptly as the ground fell away. 'Stay back from the edge,' George warned the others. 'These cliffs are high, and the rocks below are very dangerous. There's only one safe way down – the old smugglers' path.'

Anne peered nervously through the trees and could make out a wide, flat platform of grey rocks being pounded by the waves far below. She looked relieved when George led them away from the cliffs, back uphill towards the clearing where the burial barrows stood.

Carefully and silently, the five children and their dog made their way to the very edge of the clearing. They were now behind the row of high, cone-shaped tents where they had been shown the table covered in muddy shards of pottery. 'They must keep that dirty old stuff there in case anybody comes snooping around,' reasoned Julian, whispering. 'Quite clever, when you think about it. Mrs Trevelyan can pretend to be showing them what they've found in the dig, and make it look as boring as possible.'

'Where's the real treasure?' Dick asked Raymond. 'In one of the tents?'

'It was all still piled in the burial chamber last time I saw it,' the boy told him.

'Where is everybody?' wondered George in a whisper. The camp was silent and seemed to be completely deserted.

'Perhaps they've got away with the treasure already?' suggested Anne.

'But where would they go?' asked Julian. 'There's

no road leading to these woods, so they can't have a truck or even a car. And the gold must be far too heavy to carry far. Isn't that right, Raymond?' The boy nodded in agreement.

'Well then,' said Dick, 'we'd better creep in very carefully and see what's going on.'

'Yes,' Julian decided. 'We'll check for the treasure first, in case it's still inside the burial mound.'

'I'm scared!' said Anne suddenly. Something about the empty camp gave her the creeps.

'Don't worry,' her oldest brother reassured her. 'You stay here with George and Timmy.'

'I'm *not* going to be left behind!' protested George hotly. She hated being treated any differently from Julian and Dick – she could run and swim faster than either of them – and she was just as brave!

'Don't worry – we'll be back soon,' Julian assured her. 'Once we know whether the treasure's there, we can make a plan together.' Reluctantly George nodded, and Julian led Dick and a hesitant Raymond across to the low wall. They leapt over and, crouching low, dashed across the camp.

It was nearly dark now – only a watercolour smudge of crimson sunset still showed low down in the west. The three boys picked their way carefully between the high burial mounds and made their way across the planks into the deep trench that almost cut the central barrow in half. 'The chamber's at the bottom,' said Raymond, pointing. 'There's a doorway on the right.'

'I've got a torch,' said Dick, and, looking around to make sure there was still nobody in sight, he clicked it on. At the bottom of the trench was an ancient archway made of blocks of stone. Julian led the others down towards the depths of the burial mound. As they approached the stone archway, Dick's torch picked out that a stout wooden door had presumably been attached to keep out any curious people who might want to see what was inside. Mrs Trevelyan certainly didn't want any visitors suspecting that treasure had been found!

'Quietly now,' said Julian, taking the torch from Dick. He eased open the wooden door, which gave a faint creak, and they crept inside. Julian shone the light around the burial chamber and let out a gasp. A wide, low room had been constructed from huge slabs of stone. It was decorated with ornate carvings, and, here and there, paintings on the walls showed animals and scenes of warriors. Ledges and shelves were dotted around, but they had all been cleared of whatever riches they had once held. A couple of bright gold coins glittered on the floor, clearly dropped as the fake archaeologists hurried out with their spoils. In the very centre of the room was a stone sarcophagus that was also decorated with complicated carved patterns.

'This is incredible!' breathed Dick.

'But the treasure's been moved,' whispered Raymond nervously. 'I wonder where—'

But he broke off at a noise from outside. Before any of the children could do anything, there was a creak from the wooden door behind them and it was slammed firmly shut with a huge, hollow bang. Then there was a clanking noise as a padlock was fastened to the outside.

They were trapped!

12

Captured

'Let us out!' bellowed Julian, throwing himself furiously against the door, which didn't move even a fraction of an inch.

A low chuckle came from outside, muffled by the thick wood. 'Oh, I don't think so,' said the voice of Sarah Trevelyan. 'I thought you and your little gang were asking some very inconvenient questions. Babbling on about treasure and spotting our leading lights. I think it's far better if you stay locked up there until we're safely away, with the treasure.'

'You won't get away with this!' roared Dick.

'And why is that?' she asked in a mocking tone. 'Because your little friends and their doggy have gone to fetch help? It's far, far too late for that, I'm afraid. But don't worry,' her voice receded as she walked away up the wooden planks, 'when they get back, perhaps they can let you and dear Raymond out of there.'

Raymond slumped down on to the stone floor with his head in his hands. 'It's useless!' he cried. 'There's nothing we can do! They're getting away and my mother is still their prisoner!'

'No, they're not and we'll find her!' Dick told him. 'One thing you'll have to learn is that we never give up hope! Not while the others are still out there!'

Dick sat down beside Raymond and pulled the remains of the chocolate out of his pocket. Hoping to distract the scared boy, he asked, 'Why don't you tell us all about this mysterious chamber while we wait for our rescue?'

'My mother thinks this was the burial place of an important ruler from long ago,' Raymond explained with a sniff. 'A great queen of her people. She's been trying to decipher some of these carvings to find out more. But her assistant was always more interested in the gold.'

'How much gold was here?' asked Dick, running a hand over one of the empty stone shelves.

'Oh, a great deal,' said Raymond. 'Mother said it was one of the most valuable finds ever in this country. She could have become quite famous.'

'And she still will!' said Julian fiercely, filled with rage at the thought of someone's hard work being taken away from them by treachery and trickery.

George peered out into the gathering gloom as Julian and Dick hurried away, Raymond trailing behind them. Above, the trees of Whispering Wood kept up their constant, eerie rustling but she could make out no other sounds. Timmy sniffed the air and gave a small whine. 'Easy, boy,' George told him, scratching behind one ear.

For several minutes nothing happened. Then there came the distant sound of a door slamming, a muffled thumping and raised voices.

'It was a trap!' Anne whispered, looking pale and worried in the half-dark. 'They've been locked inside!'

'That Trevelyan woman must have been waiting for us,' said George with a snarl. Timmy, sensing her anger and frustration, gave a deep, rumbling growl. 'Quick, let's get over to those tents. We'll stop them getting away with the treasure if it's the last thing we do!'

'Wait!' said Anne, placing a warning hand on her arm. 'It'll be no good if we get ourselves captured too. Look!' She pointed. Sure enough, George could now see the indistinct shape of Sarah Trevelyan emerging from the trench that led through the central barrow, followed by her two henchmen, Fred and Spike.

'Move it, you two,' she ordered them. 'I reckon those other kids have gone to fetch help. Get that treasure down the smugglers' path, quick sharp! Spike, are the lights in place?'

'Don't worry,' he said with a chuckle. 'I checked 'em not half an hour ago. We'll be long gone before anybody gets here.'

'I hope you're right,' she replied, looking around at the dark trees. Her eyes passed right across the spot where George, Anne and Timmy were hiding. But the evening shadows were so deep that they were well hidden.

'I'll radio the boat then,' Sarah Trevelyan told the men. 'Hurry up with that treasure! Move it!' They disappeared inside the largest of the tents, and their boss, after one final suspicious look around the clearing, pushed open the flaps and followed.

'Now, quick!' George told Anne. And, with Timmy slinking alongside them, they scrambled over the stone wall and crept up to the back of the tent.

Inside the burial chamber, Julian pulled a penknife from his pocket and started wrestling with the wooden door. 'It's no good,' he said, slamming his hand on the stout planks in frustration. 'It's shut fast. I can feel some kind of metal bar on the outside – she must have padlocked it across.'

Dick walked to and fro, his brow furrowed in thought. His torch was balanced on one of the stone ledges. 'They must have some way of getting the treasure away,' he said, half to himself. 'What could it be?'

'We know they can't drive,' said Julian, finally giving up on the door and turning towards his brother. 'There's no road, not even a farm track.'

'So they must be going by sea,' decided Dick. 'What was it George said about getting down the cliffs?'

'Of course!' said Julian. 'The smugglers' path! George said it's the only way down! A boat must be coming to pick them up.'

'I bet that woman has gone now to radio to them,' said Dick gloomily. 'If we could get out of here, I just know we'd find a way to stop that boat. I wish Anne, George and Timmy would hurry up!'

In the large tent that served as her main headquarters, Sarah Trevelyan was looking greedily down into the two large wooden crates, standing open on a table, that held the treasure she had plundered from the Whispering Wood burial mound. The shine of gold and jewels was reflected in her eyes. Ornate necklaces, pieces of armour and delicate statues were crammed into the boxes. And on the top lay the utterly priceless golden burial mask of an ancient queen, studded with gemstones. It was an incredible piece of history, but she thought only of its value and her mouth twitched upwards into a smile.

A large radio set stood on another table to one side, and Fred was speaking urgently into the mouthpiece. 'I don't care how rough the weather looks, get to the meeting point . . . now!' There was a crackle from the radio and a voice boomed from the speaker.

'All right, all right,' it said. 'I'm on my way. Be there in half an hour. But no later! The swell's getting up, and I don't like all these rocks. Are you absolutely sure the lights are in the right place?'

'Relax, will you?' Fred told him. 'We've double checked them. See you in half an hour.' He replaced the handset on its cradle. 'He's on his way,' he told his boss.

'Excellent,' she said, tearing her gaze reluctantly away from the golden hoard. 'Put that radio out of action!' she ordered. Fred opened a panel and pulled out several small wires with a crackle and a spark.

There was an angry mumbling from the other side of the tent. 'What's that, Mrs Humphries?' asked Trevelyan, turning to face the woman who was securely tied to a solid wooden chair in the far corner. A gag was tight across her mouth, but the eyes above it burned with anger. 'Don't worry,' the thief went on. 'I can guess what you're saying. The treasure belongs in a museum, I'll never get away with it, blah blah blah. But, you see, I already have got away with it. As you just heard, my speedboat is on its way.' She slammed the lids of the two chests closed and fastened padlocks on to both of them. 'So, my old mentor, this is our farewell. Get the gold,' she told Fred and Spike. 'And let's go.'

Grunting at the weight, the two men hefted the crates by the stout rope handles on each side and followed Sarah Trevelyan as she left the tent with a mocking wave to the gagged and bound woman in the corner. But outside all three of them stopped dead. Right in their path were George and Anne with

Timmy beside them baring his white teeth and growling ferociously.

'Stop right there!' said George fiercely, 'and put that treasure back where it belongs!'

13

Timmy to the Rescue!

Sarah Trevelyan eyed the two children and the large dog calmly. 'Oh, there you are,' she said casually. 'I wondered what had happened to you two. I thought you might have run away.'

'Never!' said George, her blue eyes glinting with a steely resolve. Her family had lived in Kirrin for generations. Her blood boiled at the thought of people stealing the treasure that had lain hidden there for so long. She simply wouldn't allow it!

'It would have been much more sensible,' Trevelyan went on in the same casual drawl. 'It's so dangerous in the woods at night. You could easily get very badly hurt.' There was a glint at her side, and Anne gave a gasp of shock.

'Look out, George!' she hissed. 'She's got a gun!'

Timmy gave a loud bark and took a step forward. 'I wouldn't if I were you,' the woman warned him sharply, waving the barrel of her revolver.

George, scowling so hard it looked as if she might burst, grabbed Timmy's collar to hold him back.

Sarah Trevelyan looked back over her shoulder. 'What are you two standing there gaping for?' she scolded Fred and Spike. 'Get to the smugglers' path, quick! It's only a couple of kids! I can deal with them.' The two men struggled away with the heavy crates.

'Now,' she went on, turning back to Anne and George, 'you're not going to do anything stupid, are you?' George still looked furious, but she shook her head. She couldn't risk anything happening to Timmy. 'Good,' Trevelyan purred. She reached in her pocket and pulled out a set of keys. 'And just to prove I'm not a complete monster,' she told them, 'I'll let you release your friends and dear Raymond's mother.

But not until the morning . . .' With that, she lifted the keys and threw them far away into the trees. They vanished in the dark with a slap of leaves and a faint, distant tinkle.

Still pointing the gun at Timmy, Sarah Trevelyan backed away slowly. Once she had reached the very edge of the clearing, she turned abruptly and disappeared into the forest, following Fred, Spike and the treasure down the old smugglers' path.

'We've got to go after them!' raged George. The thought of the three robbers getting away so easily was unbearable.

'We can't!' reasoned Anne. 'She's armed! The only thing we can do is look for those keys.'

'But it's nearly night-time,' George pointed out angrily. 'We don't stand a chance of finding them until morning—'

Timmy, with a deep 'Woof!', sprinted away across the clearing. But not towards the smugglers' path. He knew better than that! Within seconds his tail had disappeared into the woods, right where the bunch of keys had been thrown.

Timmy ran full tilt through the thick undergrowth, dodging around trees and squirming under fallen branches. His sharp eyes could only see vague shapes in the gloaming, but his nose guided him with no trouble. He knew the scent of his owner's enemy very well, and he could sense it not too far away!

'Yes! Clever Tim!' said George, punching the air. 'He doesn't need light to look for something!'

George and Anne strained their eyes into the distance. They could hear Timmy moving about in the forest somewhere away to the right. 'Hurry up, Tim,' urged George quietly. 'They must be almost at the top of the cliffs by now, even carrying those heavy chests of treasure!'

Suddenly, the commotion in the undergrowth grew louder. There was a cracking of twigs, a rustling and a scurrying, and Timmy burst back out of the trees with the keys clutched firmly in his mouth.

'Good boy! Oh, good boy!' cried George as he galloped towards them.

'The *best* boy!' added Anne, stroking Timmy's silky fur. The large mongrel dropped the keys neatly in

George's hand, and she rushed straight to the main burial mound. It was almost completely dark, so she had to feel for the padlock that held the wooden door closed.

At last, George found the key that would open the padlock. Within seconds the door was open, and Julian and Dick rushed out. Raymond followed, having fetched the torch from its shelf.

'George!' Julian's voice sounded full of relief. 'We were so worried! We thought that Trevelyan woman might have hurt you!'

'I'd like to see her try,' said Anne, who had hurried up behind. 'George isn't afraid of anybody!'

'There's no time to lose!' George told Julian. 'We were listening outside their tent. They've radioed to a speedboat, and they're taking the treasure down the old smugglers' path. It'll be here in less than half an hour!'

'That's just what we thought they'd do!' exclaimed Dick.

'And your mother's inside the tent too, Raymond,' remembered Anne suddenly. 'We heard Sarah Trevelyan talking to her.'

'Well, first things first,' decided Julian. 'Let's go and set the real Mrs Humphries free. Then we'll see about that boat.'

The Five, with Raymond guiding them using the torch, raced back to the tents and burst inside the largest one. A large, empty table stood right in the centre, and over in the far corner was a woman securely fastened to a chair. Her eyes widened in surprise when she saw them, and Raymond rushed straight over with a strangled cry of 'Mother!'

'Give me those keys,' Dick told George. He sprinted across to the back of the chair, where another padlock held the ropes and chains in place. The first key he tried unlocked it, and Hannah Humphries was free. She tore the gag from her mouth and embraced her son. 'Raymond!' she cried out. 'I've been so worried! How on earth did you escape?'

'With a little help from my friends,' he told her, standing up and turning proudly to the Five. 'This is Julian, Dick, Anne, George – and Timmy, of course.'

'I owe you a huge amount of thanks,' said the

archaeologist, getting to her feet. 'What brave children. And what a wonderful dog!'

'Wuff!' agreed Timmy.

'It's jolly decent of Raymond to call us his friends,' said Dick, blushing. 'I'm afraid we weren't all very good to him.'

'No, we weren't,' admitted Julian. 'We thought you were unhappy about spending time with us, you see. We never dreamt you'd been threatened to keep quiet by those awful robbers!'

'Well, it all seems to have worked out for the best,' said Mrs Humphries with a small smile, before sadly adding, 'I'm only sorry we aren't in time to save the treasure.'

'Oh, yes we are!' Everybody in the tent turned to look at George.

'Listen carefully, all of you,' she said. 'I've got a plan.'

14

The Leading Lights

Ever since she had discovered that Trevelyan and her henchmen were escaping by sea, George had been thinking furiously. How on earth were these crooks hoping to get through Kirrin Bay in a speedboat in the middle of the night? Trying to navigate would be terribly dangerous. The water was full of unpredictable tides and currents and the spiky rocks could sink a boat within seconds.

And now, she had finally hit on the answer.

She rushed to the table in the middle of the tent, grabbed a piece of folded paper from her pocket and smoothed it out on the wooden surface.

'George, how's that going to help?' said Dick. 'That's your sea chart of Kirrin Bay . . .'

'Remember those lights we saw from Kirrin Island?' said George. 'I know what they must be. They're leading lights!'

'Leading lights!' echoed Dick, his eyes shining with excitement. 'Of course! We heard Sarah Trevelyan mention something about them after she locked us up.'

'What are they?' asked Anne.

'They're lights that are put up to show boats a safe route,' George explained. 'All you have to do is keep the two lights in a straight line. Look!' She pointed to the place where Whispering Wood was marked on her map, before moving her finger out to sea. 'The speedboat needs to stay well away from the rocks,' she explained, 'so they must have plotted a safe path.'

'So all they need to do is keep the lights in line, one above the other, and they'll get clean away?' asked Anne.

George grinned across at her cousin. 'That's what *would* happen, yes, if everything went as they planned . . . But what if one of the lights moved? They'd go in the wrong direction. And instead of steering *around* the rocks, we could send those thieves right in among them!'

'Brilliant!' said Julian, poring over the chart. 'Yes, here,' he said, pointing. 'You can see the island here and the rocks. So, they must be following a line *here* to the western side of the bay.' He traced a line with his finger. 'Where exactly were those lights?'

'The first one we saw was right on the clifftop, wasn't it?' remembered Anne. She pointed. 'Here.'

'That's right,' said George. 'That was the one lower down – the red one. And the other green one must be here, on that hill.'

'Then, all we need to do is move that second lantern to the left,' said Dick, also studying George's map carefully, 'and they'll never be able to get away!'

'But won't they be hurt?' asked Anne, looking worried.

'If they were, it would serve them right!' said Julian, looking stern. 'But no. They'll have life jackets in the boat and we can quickly sail out and make sure they don't get into too much trouble. But we'll also make sure they don't steal that treasure!'

Soon, the plan was made. Anne and Julian would go through the wood and move the leading light to throw the speedboat off course. Dick and George would rush as fast as they could down to their own boat, with Timmy, and sail out to the rescue.

'And Raymond and I will go and fetch the police as quickly as we can!' said Mrs Humphries shakily.

'Then it's settled,' said Julian. 'Good luck! Just tell them that the Famous Five are in the middle of another adventure – and we'll have some thieves ready for them to arrest if they come straight to Kirrin Island!' With a nod, Raymond and his mother disappeared out of the tent.

'Good luck, everyone!' said Julian. 'Anne, you come with me!' And he led his sister out of the clearing, shining the beam of his torch into the trees.

'This way,' Anne told him, catching sight of a glow through the trees. 'I can see it! Up at the top of that rise.' Together they climbed through the dark wood, surrounded by fluttering and scuffling as the night-time creatures of the forest were disturbed by these giant invaders. At one point an owl swooped low in front of them, a ghostly white shape dipping in and out of the torch beam.

'There it is!' said Julian after a time, looking up through the branches and seeing the bright light. They dashed over and discovered that a lantern ringed with green glass had been hung some way up a stout oak tree. 'Hold the torch,' Julian instructed, and began to climb.

It didn't take him long to reach the lantern. He looked away to his left – and identified another tree of a similar height, silhouetted by the moon and stars not far away. 'That should be perfect,' he said to himself, remembering George's map. He unhooked the lantern and climbed back down.

'I say, Anne,' he said as he carried the lantern through the wood, 'do you know what I just realised? We wouldn't have solved this mystery if you hadn't worked out that woman wasn't Raymond's real mother. That was jolly clever!'

'Like I said,' Anne blushed, 'it's not about discovering

secret passageways. Sometimes you have to find out something about *people* too.'

'In any case, you're definitely the hero of this adventure. I just hope we're not too late!' He arrived at the foot of the other tall tree. 'Here,' he decided, 'this should do perfectly.'

'You'll have to hurry!' said Anne. 'Listen!'

Out to sea beneath the high cliffs at the edge of the wood, they could hear the roar of a powerful motor.

It was hard climbing with the lantern slung over one of his arms, but Julian was tall and strong. He heaved himself upwards through the foliage until he found a stout branch at about the right height. Sitting on it, he stuck his penknife firmly into the trunk and hung the leading light from it. 'There,' he said as he rejoined Anne on the forest floor. 'That ought to do it.'

Above them, the green light shone out brightly across the forest, just as before. But this time it was in a very different place. Instead of marking a safe route out to sea, any boat trying to use these leading lights would be sent straight towards the sharp rocks that stuck out of the sea like jagged teeth, hidden among the waves that danced and rippled in the moonlit bay.

Guardians of Kirrin Island

At the base of the cliffs, the night-time sea sucked and sloshed across the flat grey rocks. The moon cast a pale, sickly light across the water as a wooden motorboat made its cautious, slow approach to the coast. The red and green leading lights up in Whispering Wood had helped the captain steer safely through the rocks in the bay, but he knew this was still a dangerous place to land. His eyes searched carefully for a narrow passageway that led into the platform of rock; a natural harbour just big enough for a small boat. Carefully, he nudged the prow of his launch into this opening and hopped out on to the slippery rocks.

Halfway up the cliffs he could make out the bobbing light of a torch as Sarah Trevelyan and her two helpers made their way down the old smugglers' path with the second chest full of stolen treasure. The first was placed securely on a low rocky ledge not far away. The man began to pace backwards and forwards, willing the figures in the dark above him to hurry up.

Not far away, Dick and George were dashing over the common, back towards Kirrin Village. Timmy raced ahead of them – now *this* was more like it. He had spent far too much of the night being made to keep quiet and was delighted to be able to run. He gave a bark of delight. 'That's right, Tim,' said George encouragingly. 'You show us the way! Back to the boat – quick as you can!'

Kirrin Cottage lay away to their left, but the children took a more direct route down to the beach. Soon they were racing along a narrow, cobbled street, and out on to the shore. There was their boat, safely dragged up on to the sand and securely anchored as usual. Timmy jumped in, and Dick and George set about pushing the boat into the water.

'It's getting late, but the water's still lovely and warm!' said Dick. 'It's a fine time for a moonlight swim!'

'Let's hope so,' said George, and her teeth flashed white in the darkness as she gave a wolfish grin. 'Because that's what those thieves are going to get in a few moments!'

A brisk offshore breeze was blowing, and as soon as George pulled on a rope to raise the sail, the boat lurched forward through the water like a horse being spurred on in a race. Timmy stood right at the front with his tail up and his ears blowing in the wind as the boat surged out into the bay.

On the rocks at the foot of the cliff, Spike and Fred hefted the second of the weighty wooden chests into the motorboat, which settled even lower in the water.

'Hey!' protested the captain. 'What's in there, anyway? I never got told nothing about a cargo this heavy! We'll be swamped!'

'Don't be ridiculous,' Sarah Trevelyan told him coolly. 'You've been well paid to take us out to the ship, and we've supplied you with a safe route through the rocks. These waves aren't too rough yet. We'll be fine.'

Grumbling, the man untied the rope and pushed on a button. With a cough and a sputter, the outboard motor sprang into life.

Sarah Trevelyan took one final look up at the cliffs. 'That's the last time I'll have to be an assistant to anybody,' she said to herself with satisfaction. With a chuckle, she leapt nimbly into the boat. 'Let's go,' she told the man in the stern.

The boat edged out into the sea slowly. 'Come on,' grumbled Spike. 'I thought this was supposed to be a powerful boat. Give it some speed!'

'I can't see the bleeding lights yet, can I?' said the captain rudely. 'We need to get a bit further out until I've got both lights in view – and that's the only way to get safely through the rocks. A fine mess we'd be in if I steer straight into one of those, especially with this heavy stuff on board!' He continued to putter slowly away from the cliffs, the boat rocking sharply from side to side in the growing swell.

Dick heard a *put-put-put* noise from away beneath the cliffs. 'George!' he hissed. 'They've started the motor! I can hear them!'

'Good!' said George, and Timmy gave his own low growl of satisfaction. George steered them expertly, keeping Kirrin Island on their right, before making a turn and heading out across the head of the bay. Soon, she turned the boat into the wind so they came to a gentle halt.

'What now?' asked Dick.

'Now,' said George with another grin, 'we wait.' In the distance, she could see the red and green lights shining in the forest.

The same lights were also now in view from the motorboat. 'At last,' said the captain in relief, and turned the boat along the coast until the lights were exactly in line – the green one above the red. 'Hold on,' he told the other three. 'I've got the route now, so we'll head out to sea.'

Sarah Trevelyan sat on one side of the boat, her hand resting on the two wooden chests packed with the treasure from the Whispering Wood barrows.

Spike sat on the other side, and Fred in the prow. 'Ready,' she told the captain, and he pushed on a lever. The putter of the motor rose to a roar. The back of the boat dipped low in the water as it quickly picked up speed, and soon it was racing out to sea, the captain keeping his eyes firmly fixed behind them, making sure the lights stayed exactly in line.

By the time the boat approached the rocks around Kirrin Island, it was going very fast. Fred, at the front of the boat, saw the blackness of a shard of rock rushing towards them and turned to shout out a warning, but it was too late. With a hideous crunch, the boat ran straight on to a cluster jutting out of the sea. It was already so low in the water that it began to go down within seconds.

All four passengers were wearing life jackets, so they weren't in any danger. But the heavy chests full of treasure could not be saved. Sarah Trevelyan tried desperately to grab one of the rope handles, but the crate began to pull her under and she quickly had to let go. The boat and its cargo vanished without a

trace into the dark waters of Kirrin Bay, and those on board were left stranded in the midnight sea, spluttering and shivering with shock.

'Looks like your little robbery hasn't gone quite to plan!' sang out a merry voice across the dark water. It was answered by a laugh and a deep bark.

'Who's there?' said Sarah in shock. 'Who is it?'

'Surprised to see us?' said Dick as the dim shape of their boat came into view. 'After all, you did lock us away in a burial mound earlier. Luckily for you, we're back!'

'Watch out for the rocks!' said the captain.

'I rather think it's *you* that needed that particular warning,' George told him cheerfully. 'Then you wouldn't have had to use those rather unreliable leading lights, would you?'

'You . . .' spluttered Sarah Trevelyan, taking in a mouthful of salty water in her shock. 'You changed the lights! You stopped us getting away! You meddling little—'

'Now, now,' said Dick. 'I should watch your language, if I were you! Kirrin Island isn't far away

– and if you behave yourselves, you can wait for the police there rather than in the water.'

'And if you ever decide to try and steal someone else's treasure again,' added George, 'you'd better make sure you don't do it anywhere near the Famous Five!'

'WOOF!' agreed Timmy, wagging his tail.

FIFTY-FIVE
YEARS
LATER . . .

16

A Plot – and a Plan

Fran's first thought when she woke up was *I must have been dreaming*. There was no way that she had really escaped from a cottage with a mysterious old professor, followed a secret passageway, spent the night in the woods out in the open air and been told a story about lost, sunken treasure. She must've fallen asleep with her head full of adventure.

But, almost immediately, the sound of whispering leaves overhead and the birdsong told her she hadn't been dreaming. It had all been real. Fran opened her eyes.

Bright sunlight was filtering through the fresh green leaves overhead, filling the clearing with a soft, golden light. She was lying on a soft bed of bracken in a quilted sleeping bag, with Gilbert tucked up, warm and comforting, in the crook of her legs. Maddy and Tom lay not far away, still apparently fast asleep.

There was the crunch of footsteps nearby and George came into view, carrying an armful of sticks. 'Good morning,' she said quietly, seeing that Fran was awake. She knelt beside the fire and began gently blowing on some of the still-hot embers right at the centre, feeding them with a few small sticks. By the time Fran had sat up, stretched and rubbed her eyes, a cheerful fire was starting to blaze.

'There's a stream just over there if you want to wash your face,' said George, pointing out of the clearing. Fran padded off, Gilbert beside her, and found a fresh, sparkling spring gushing out of a mossy bank. The dog lapped thirstily at the water and Fran used her cupped hands to splash some on her face. She gasped – the water was so cold and refreshing. 'Better than a cup of tea, eh?' said George as Fran re-entered the forest clearing. 'Although there will be actual breakfast in twenty minutes or so. We've got a busy day ahead.'

'What are we doing?' asked Fran, her head still fuzzy from sleep despite the cold spring water.

'Saving the treasure, of course!' exclaimed George, placing a small camping kettle carefully over the flames. 'Didn't you listen to the story last night?'

'I did,' came a voice from behind them, 'and I have a few questions.' Maddy had now woken up, and was sitting upright, leaning back against one of the cut logs with her sleeping bag wrapped around her legs.

'What kind of questions?' George wanted to know.

'Well,' said Maddy, 'how long have you got? Because there are a lot of questions about a group of kids going off to live on an island, completely unsupervised, for a start. Plus, creeping about in the woods in the dead of night and causing a boat to actually sink. I mean, you're making it up, right?'

'I never tell lies,' replied George, with an angry flash deep in her blue eyes. 'This was a long time ago, remember. A lot of things have changed since then. Children have certainly changed! Not many of them will have spent the night outdoors like you.'

'Although it was surprisingly comfortable,' said a fourth voice. Tom was now awake too, lying on his back looking up at the blue sky through the leaves. 'You know what? I think I could get used to living like the . . . what did you call yourselves? The Famous Five?'

'We didn't call ourselves that for a long while,' said George with a smile, 'but then one day a police officer made up that nickname for us and it stuck.'

'Well,' said Tom, 'I'm in. Bring me my ginger beer and sign me up for the Famous Five!'

'We didn't drink ginger beer *all* the time, you know,' George told him, before turning back to Maddy. 'You said you had some questions?'

'I do,' said Maddy, looking serious again. 'What did you mean, when you said we were going to save the treasure? Do you really mean the treasure from the story?'

'Of course!' said George. 'Why on earth do you think Raymond came back to get the map?'

'Raymond!' said Fran in shock. 'What? The kid who stayed with you on Kirrin Island?'

'Who else?' said George. With a sigh, she sat down and looked at them all with a sad expression. 'I didn't tell you what happened after the story.' She straightened her shoulders. 'Right, so you remember what happened to the treasure?'

'It sank and was lost?' asked Tom.

'It did sink, yes,' said George. 'But it wasn't quite lost. I know those rocks like the back of my hand, so even in the dark that night, I managed to see exactly where their boat went down. But then I did something I'm not proud of, I'm afraid.'

'What?' asked Fran, startled by the mournful and regretful expression the professor was now wearing beneath her grey curls.

'When the police asked where the treasure had sunk,' George said softly, 'I told them the wrong location. I knew that if people thought there was sunken treasure close to Kirrin Island, it would be swamped with those hoping to find it. It's happened before, you see. I pretended that the chests had gone down to the seabed much further out. Some did search for a while, but they soon gave up. It's far too deep and dark to find anything further out in the bay, and everybody soon forgot about it.'

'Except Raymond!' Maddy broke in.

'Yes,' said George, 'except him. Over the years he kept turning up every now and then, insisting I must know more about where the boat sank. He knew I had that map showing the rocks, and I think he guessed I would have noted down where the wreck was.'

'He didn't seem like such a bad guy in the past, though,' Fran reasoned. 'A bit wimpy and cowardly, maybe.'

'I think that's exactly what he is,' George told her. 'Just look at that poor dog who trails around after him. If you really want to know about someone, take a look at their dog.' Her eyes had a faraway look for a moment. 'But he turned up a few weeks ago, saying he owed a lot of money to some very nasty people. He wanted me to help him dive for the treasure and he offered to split the profits with me.'

'And you told him to get lost, I bet,' said Maddy with a smile.

'I certainly did,' replied George, 'and not as politely as that either! Imagine the publicity if sunken treasure gets found here. Day-trippers and reporters and all the rest of it snooping around *my* island.' She got to her feet and paced up and down angrily.

'But Raymond didn't take no for an answer?' Tom prompted her.

'I didn't realise how desperate he must be,' George admitted. 'He was back at Kirrin Cottage yesterday telling me he simply must have the treasure. Spouted a load of stuff about this being my final warning and how he wouldn't be responsible for the consequences if I refused to give him the map.'

'He's being threatened by someone,' Fran realised. She couldn't help feeling a small stab of pity for Raymond. Just like in George's story, he seemed to cut a rather weak, pathetic figure. 'Remember the man we saw at the window?'

'Raymond called him Clay.' Maddy remembered the man with his cold, pale eyes.

'That's right,' said George. 'He must be the real brains behind all this – and the one pulling Raymond's strings. His goons were supposed to keep us in Kirrin Cottage while their little puppet went to go and fetch the treasure for them.'

'But now we've escaped!' said Fran.

'Indeed we have,' George agreed. 'And if you still think you're ready for an adventure, you can come with me to Kirrin Island, and stop him from leaving with the gold.'

'It's a big yes from me!' said Tom, getting out of his sleeping bag and capering around the clearing. 'Get that tea brewing, and let's go adventuring! The new Famous Five to the rescue!'

George chuckled. 'I'm not sure whether we'll ever be quite as famous as the originals,' she said. Then she added, with tears in her eyes as she looked around at the three children and the dog, 'Although I must say . . . it is rather nice to be Five again.'

17

Five on a Secret Trail

KEEP OUT — CCTV IN OPERATION — GUARD DOGS ON
PATROL — NO ENTRY — DANGER! FALLING ROCKS read
the large red sign stuck in the chalky soil at the edge
of the quarry.

'Slight overkill on the warning messages?' asked
Maddy drily as George led them past the sign and
down the rocky slope. The quarry was a deep
depression in the ground, not far from the edge of
Whispering Wood and near the clifftops above Kirrin.

'Don't know what you're talking about,' George
told her with what might have been a wink. 'Watch

your step here!' The three children and Gilbert followed her gingerly down to the very bottom of the dip. Gorse bushes, thistles and nettles grew thickly among the stones, and it was difficult to avoid getting pricked or stung as they walked along the bottom of the gully towards a large, flat stone that stuck out near the base of the slope. Beneath this stone was a solid-looking metal door bolted into the hillside.

'Just in case the signs aren't enough to keep the snoopers away,' George explained, pulling a bunch of keys out of her pocket. She rummaged for the correct key, then used it to unlock the metal door. It swung open inwards on well-oiled hinges.

'Clay and his men must know we've escaped from Kirrin Cottage,' George explained, 'so it's odds on that they'll be watching the coast in case we try and get to the island to stop Raymond or send the police after him. But I'll bet they don't know about this. Almost nobody does except me and your grandad and the rest of the original Five. Watch your heads! You have to crawl the first bit, then it gets easier.' And with that, the professor dropped to her hands and knees and vanished nimbly into the darkness.

'What now?' asked Fran.

'I guess we follow the human rabbit,' said Tom with a shrug. 'Come on!' And he crouched down and crawled through the opening. With a shrug, Maddy followed him.

Fran looked uncertainly at the dark doorway. She wasn't great with confined spaces. But after a moment there was a shout from Tom. 'Come on!' said his echoing voice. 'You're not going to believe this!' She placed a hand on Gilbert's collar for reassurance, and together the girl and her dog wriggled their way into the narrow passage.

Once she had made her way down the tunnel for a little while, Fran was relieved to find that it widened out into a much larger passageway. In the dim light from the distant doorway behind her, she could see Maddy and Tom standing with George.

'Another secret passage?' Maddy was asking. 'How on earth did you discover it?'

'It was a friend of mine who discovered it, actually,'

said George. And she reached down and absent-mindedly scratched Gilbert behind the ears. 'The best friend I ever had.'

'A dog?' realised Fran. 'Was it Timmy? From the story?'

'Yes,' said George sadly. 'Good old Tim.' She sniffed and wiped her eye.

'Why didn't you get another dog?' Fran asked quietly, patting George on the arm.

'There'll never be another Timmy,' said George shortly, wiping another tear away. She visibly pulled herself together. 'Right,' she told the children, 'let's focus. Raymond might find the treasure at any moment. We'll have to be quick.' She reached out to the right-hand wall and pulled down a lever on a grey box set into the wall. There was a dull clunk, and a series of bare bulbs strung along the wall on a wire began to light up, one by one. They led away as the passageway sloped steeply downwards.

'Does this lead to the island?' asked Maddy with a gasp.

'It does,' George replied. 'This tunnel links up with the undersea caves.'

'Under . . . sea?' repeated Fran nervously.

'As in caves that are actually, you know . . . beneath the water?' Tom wanted to know.

'Don't worry,' George told him kindly. 'You said you wanted an adventure, remember? Come on!' And she set off at a brisk pace down the tunnel, following the string of softly glowing bulbs.

'Anyone else having second thoughts about this adventure business already?' moaned Tom.

After they had walked steeply downwards for what seemed to Tom's weary legs like hours, but was more like twenty minutes, the carved rock of the tunnel merged into a series of caves. It was much colder down here, and the pale walls dripped with condensation. Here and there, other openings led to different passageways, but the string of lights led them safely onwards. 'You wouldn't want to get lost down here,' George called back over her shoulder, her voice echoing creepily back through the tunnels: *lost down here . . . lost down here . . . lost . . . lost . . .* Fran shivered and even Gilbert let out a meek whimper.

Presently the floor began to change from rock to sand, and the caves began to climb again. They went from one level to another using wooden stairs that had been built to help. 'Did you do this?' Maddy asked George.

'Of course,' replied the professor. 'Nobody else is allowed in my caves – or on my island. I told you! Ah, here's my father's old workroom!' They had come out into a much larger cave. Old wooden tables were scattered about, as well as some very rusty pieces of what seemed to be scientific equipment.

'Do you do the same kind of research as your father?' Maddy asked, stopping to examine an old leather notebook. She turned over a couple of pages filled with numbers and symbols written in cramped, spidery handwriting.

'I do,' George confirmed. 'He had some brilliant ideas but could never quite get the experiments to work. He wanted to discover a clean source of energy without having to rely on oil or gas. He was a long, long way ahead of his time. Not that any of us realised,' she added sadly in an undertone, sighing and looking around the chamber. 'Well, no time for that now,' decided George. 'Come on, it's this way.'

Once again, they followed the lights, which led them up and up until they were in a tunnel that seemed to have been made by humans rather than a natural cavern. Eventually a wall of gigantic grey stones appeared on their left. 'The castle dungeons are behind there,' George told them. 'We need to be quiet from now on. I'm sure Raymond won't know about this passage; it isn't marked on my map. But we should still be careful.'

Silently the five of them crept up one final flight of stone stairs. It seemed to come to a halt beside a sheer wall of ancient bricks, but George reached into an opening high up in the wall and triggered some hidden mechanism. With a soft clunk, a section of the wall swung backwards and blinding sunlight spilt into the passageway. Holding a finger to her lips, George peered out of the opening, and then jumped – immediately vanishing from sight.

'I wish she wouldn't keep disappearing like that!' whispered Tom to Fran.

Suddenly George's curly head reappeared. 'Coast is clear,' she told them softly. 'Follow me, but stay low and keep Gilbert quiet! If he's anything like my Timmy, he won't be able to resist chasing the rabbits.'

One by one, the children lowered themselves out of the opening in the wall, squinting against the bright light, which after an hour or more underground made their eyes smart. After a few moments Fran's eyes began to adjust and she looked around.

They were standing in a gigantic fireplace, easily big enough for a fully-grown adult to stand up in. It was set into the thick wall of an ancient stone room, but the rest of the building was ruined, and large stones had tumbled here and there. Craning her neck forward, Fran could see a high castle tower rising above them, with black birds circling the top and uttering sharp cries of '*chack, chack, chack*'. On the other side of the wall was a wide castle courtyard, surrounded by more ruined rooms. Rabbits hopped fearlessly on the sandy ground, and the coconut-biscuit scent of gorse flowers filled the warm air.

George smiled at her. 'Welcome to Kirrin Island.'

18

The Mystery of Kirrin Cave

'Remember to stay low,' George told the three children. 'This way!' She moved cautiously to the other side of the room and peered around the castle courtyard. The rabbits watched her curiously. 'Clear,' she mouthed, and beckoned them forward. Together they crept quickly across the courtyard, climbing through a large gap in the ruined castle wall opposite, and up to a sandy slope between some gorse bushes that led to a low hill. Kirrin Village was now visible in the distance, with brightly dressed tourists filling the sandy beach. The dark shape of Whispering Wood loomed on the clifftops.

Still looking carefully in all directions, George led them to the very top of the hill and squeezed carefully between two of the larger bushes. Carefully avoiding the sharp thorns, they followed to find her lifting up a wooden hatch set into the ground. 'I put this here a few years back,' she said, 'in case anybody came snooping. I wouldn't want them finding the cave by accident.'

Maddy gasped. 'Is this the one you discovered all those years ago?' she asked.

'Of course,' said George. 'We'll go one by one! I'll bring you, boy.' She scooped Gilbert up under one arm, and he was too startled to protest. George sat on the edge of the opening and, with her other hand, reached for a rope-ladder that dangled from the cave roof. 'We used to use a bit of knotted rope,' she explained, 'but I find this easier these days.' And she swung herself deftly down, landing with a thump on the sandy floor. Tom followed, then Maddy, and Fran brought up the rear, carefully closing the wooden hatch behind her.

The cave looked out over the rocks at the back of Kirrin Island. It was airy and cool, and felt immediately

welcoming, almost as if it had been waiting for them. 'You still come out here?' asked Maddy, looking around her. There was a large cool box and a kitbag stashed on a natural shelf of rock in one corner.

'Why wouldn't I?' asked George, rummaging in the bag and bringing out a small camping stove.

'Well, you know, you're a . . . a grown-up,' said Maddy. 'Grown-ups don't normally go on adventures to deserted islands.'

'More's the pity,' replied George with a sniff. 'I come here all the time. This island has been my second home since long before you were born. Now, we'll sneak out in a moment and see where Raymond's hiding himself. But first and most importantly . . .' She turned the little plastic handle on the stove. There was a clicking and a small *whumf* as a blue flame sparked into life. 'Another cup of tea.' She fetched a kettle from the bag and a bottle of water from the cool box.

'Are hot drinks a major part of this process then?' Tom wanted to know.

'All good adventures start with a cup of tea,' George told him.

A few minutes later, Fran sat at the edge of the cave, staring out over the bright bay as she cradled a steaming tin mug in her hands. A fresh breeze blew her dark hair away from her face with a tang of salt and a refreshing smack of sea spray.

'It's not so bad, is it, this adventuring business?' asked Tom, coming to sit beside her. 'I think I could get used to it.'

'Definitely,' said Fran, feeling a strange mixture of contentment and excitement as she watched the endless waves churning towards them and pondered what was about to happen. How was George planning to save the treasure?

'Right,' said George soon afterwards. 'Time to see what Raymond is up to and how he's going to recover those heavy chests. He must have landed by boat in the cove. If we sneak through the castle, we can spy on him from the other side. Let's go, carefully and quietly!'

They each climbed back up the rope-ladder, with George carrying Gilbert again, which made Fran smile. After hearing about the much-missed Timmy, she understood a little more about George's previous refusal to have a dog in the house. The memories must be far too painful.

The five of them crept so stealthily through the castle courtyard that Tom felt he could have reached out and petted some of the rabbits. Gilbert had other plans, but a warning look from George told him that wasn't allowed.

George held a finger to her lips and dropped down on to her tummy. Copying her, they all wriggled softly up a sandy slope and reached the top of a low rise between two high patches of sea grass. There, to their right, was a small cove with a sleek white motorboat pulled up on to the golden sand. The beach was littered with equipment: metal gas canisters of different sizes, coils of wire, a selection of hooks and a few strange white pieces of material. A wetsuit was draped over the side of the boat, and nearby Raymond Humphries sat on a metal case, his head bent over a piece of paper. His dog lay nearby, its tail down and head between its paws.

'He's got the map!' said Maddy in a whisper. As they looked, Raymond picked up a small device that had been sitting next to him. He tapped a few buttons on a keypad.

'What's he got there?' wondered Tom.

'Some kind of GPS device, I'm guessing,' said George. 'He's trying to pinpoint the exact site of the shipwreck. Why did I mark it on the map?'

'You weren't expecting the map to be stolen,' Maddy told her kindly. 'But anyway – how is he going to get the treasure even if he does find it? He'll never lift it to the surface.'

'I'm not sure,' said George. 'I've never seen some of that equipment before. But he must think he can recover it, or he wouldn't have gone to all this trouble.' Suddenly there was a fizzing noise from the beach, and a crackly voice said, 'Are you there? Come in!'

Raymond leapt up and opened the cover of the box he was sitting on. It contained a powerful-looking radio, and he grabbed a handset. 'Yes, I'm here,' he answered irritably.

'Do you have the treasure yet, my friend?' came the quiet, calm tones of the man called Clay.

'Give me a chance!' Raymond looked frightened. 'It's only been light for an hour,' he said in a wheedling tone. 'I'm just pinpointing the wreck, then I'll dive. You'll have your money, don't worry.'

'I'm not worried for myself,' came Clay's voice, 'only for you. I've made it clear what will happen if you don't fetch me that treasure. But there's a complication. Professor Kirrin and those children seem to have disappeared.'

'What?' Raymond almost dropped the radio. 'How did they get away?'

There was a pause and another crackle of static. Then Clay spoke again. 'It seems I may have . . . underestimated the professor. She caused a diversion last night and we can't locate her.'

'What if they've gone for the police?' whined Raymond.

'All the more reason for you to hurry up and get that treasure. We'll be at the bottom of the smugglers' path, as agreed, in precisely two hours. Don't be late, Raymond. You know what'll happen if you let us down.' The radio clicked off.

Raymond got to his feet in a panic. 'Get in the boat!' he ordered the dog, pointing. Still with its tail down, it obeyed him. Raymond spent the next ten minutes rushing around, frantically loading up his gear. Then he pulled on the wetsuit, pushed the boat into the shallow water and leapt in. He spent a moment looking intently at his GPS device, then pressed a button to start the engine. Steering carefully, he sailed out of the cove and was soon lost to sight around the far headland. He left some of the canisters and the radio behind.

'He's going to dive for the treasure!' said Maddy. 'And we don't have a boat to go and stop him! He'll get away!'

'He might find the treasure,' said George, standing up and brushing the sand from her jeans, 'but he won't escape. Not on my watch – and certainly not on *my* island!'

19

The Shipwreck

Half a mile away from Kirrin Island, deep beneath the water, where weed waved lazily among the numerous sharp rocks that jutted up from the seabed, the wreck of a motorboat had lain undiscovered for more than fifty years. This far down, the rays of the summer sun hardly reached it. The water here was cold, and the timbers of the old boat had been well preserved. Crabs and small fish darted in and out of the seaweed that had grown across the forgotten hulk. Forgotten, that is, by most people. But not quite everyone.

The waves of dancing sunlight far overhead rippled and parted as the shadow of a boat passed across the surface, picking its way carefully among the rocks. A splash in the sea shattered the sunbeams into shimmering diamonds and a black anchor came snaking its way down to the seabed, dragging a long chain behind it. Soon there was a second splash up on the surface, and a diver came, pulling himself carefully downwards by the anchor chain. The fish and crabs scattered as he clicked on a powerful underwater torch, playing its beam across the dark seabed.

The diver hesitated a few metres from the bottom and peered all around, unclipping a small electronic device from his belt and checking his location. Then he let go of the chain and kicked off, making for the darker area beneath a large overhang of rock. It was here, in the shadows, that he found what he was looking for.

There was nobody there to see, but the diver's eyes widened behind his mask, and a dancing cloud of bubbles surged upwards as his breathing quickened.

Adjusting a valve on his arm, he drifted gently downwards until his flippers came to rest on the wrecked boat. It was lying on its side, and he had to climb awkwardly down into it to search properly.

One of the wooden chests was still inside the boat. The other had rolled a little way across the ocean floor. But both were intact. Working quickly now, the diver began to pull more things from his loaded belt. He criss-crossed wires and firmly fixed them round each of the chests, then he unfolded two large white objects and fastened them to the wire with metal clips. Finally, he pulled out a small canister and fixed it to one of the white shapes. There was a hiss and it inflated – revealing itself to be a large balloon. Slowly at first, but quickly picking up speed, the first chest left its resting place and rose to the surface. A couple of minutes later, the second one followed.

With one last look around, the diver kicked himself upwards using the anchor chain for support. The sunlight on the surface broke into shards as he climbed back into the boat. With a puff of sand, the anchor was pulled from the seabed and hoisted away and the

shadow of the boat, towing the two balloons behind it with the bobbing chests hanging underneath, slowly disappeared from view. The old, wrecked boat was left in peace once again – this time for good.

Up in the speedboat, Raymond pulled off his diving mask and wiped his face with the palm of his hand. For most of his life he had dreamt of this lost treasure – the treasure his mother had discovered – forgotten at the bottom of the sea. And now he had finally tracked it down. His smile vanished from his face almost straight away, though, as he remembered the hardened criminals who would be waiting for him at the foot of the cliffs. The men he was heavily in debt to – and who would take most of this treasure away from him. He shrugged his shoulders. There was enough gold in the chests behind him to clear all his debts and allow him to make a fresh start. Raymond pressed the button to start the outboard motor, preparing to head back to shore.

Nothing happened.

Not far away, on Kirrin Island, George was lying on her stomach near the entrance to the cave. She was holding a strange device that looked like a long grey box. It had a cone at one end, and a series of moving dials and blinking lights along the side. George was staring at the boat through a scope on top.

'What did you do?' asked Maddy, who was lying beside her.

'I've disabled the electronics in his boat,' said George in a satisfied tone. 'He won't be able to start the engine now. He'll have to head back to the island for repairs. And we'll be waiting for him!'

'See?' said Tom. 'Some of your inventions work.'

'Hey!' George grunted, but with a slight smile in her eyes.

Back in the boat, Raymond sweated and cursed as he mashed the button. His dog cowered in the stern. Eventually, with a muttered oath, Raymond picked up an oar from the bottom of the boat and began to scull back towards Kirrin Island. 'I'll have to radio them and tell them to get another boat,' he told himself crossly. He was so lost in his thoughts that he didn't see the five figures on the clifftop until he was almost directly beneath them. Silhouetted by the afternoon sun, George, Maddy, Fran, Tom and Gilbert were watching the boat as it approached.

'Ah, you used balloons to float the treasure chests, did you?' called George. 'Very clever. I wondered what those were.'

'So, you made it out to the island after all, did you, *Georgina*?' shouted Raymond. His dog whimpered as he stood up, making the boat rock alarmingly from side to side.

'We certainly did,' came the reply. 'But you seem to be having some trouble with your boat's engine. Shame. You can't load up the gold and escape now, can you?'

'And I suppose you think you're going to stop me?' taunted Raymond. 'A washed-up old scientist, just like your weird dad, and three kids?'

'And a dog!' added Fran hotly. Gilbert gave a 'Wuff!' of agreement.

'Oh, yes.' Raymond's mouth twisted in a cruel smile. 'You like dogs, don't you, George? Well, here you go! This should slow you down a bit!' And, desperate to create some kind of diversion, he picked up his own dog and flung it into the sea. It splashed into the water with a frightened yelp of panic.

George didn't hesitate. As Raymond dug his oar into the water, rowing for the shore as hard as he could, she threw herself from the clifftop in a perfect dive. She had been a strong swimmer all her life, and it didn't take her long to reach the terrified, thrashing dog.

Maddy, meanwhile, dashed off down the hill towards the castle. 'Come on!' she called to Fran and Tom. 'We've got to stop him!' They raced after her, through the castle courtyard with such speed that this time the rabbits all scattered with a flurry of bobbing white tails. They skidded on the sandy floor as they turned through the gatehouse and sprinted to the cove.

Raymond's boat was already there, its prow buried in the sand. And, as they approached, he leapt out of the front of the boat swinging the wooden oar at them threateningly.

'Stay back,' he ordered them. 'I'm warning you!'

'It's over, Raymond!' Maddy shouted back. 'Your boat's out of action; you have to give up!'

'Says who?' he jeered, coming closer to them and

swinging the oar so they had to jump backwards. 'You four can't stop me!'

'For the last time,' said Fran, 'we're not four. We're five!' And, at that moment, Gilbert came galloping down the slope between the children and leapt fearlessly at Raymond with his teeth bared.

Raymond fell down backwards, dropping the oar in surprise.

'Yeah! The *Famous* Five!' Maddy raced down the beach and kicked the oar away.

'New edition!' added Tom.

But Raymond wasn't defeated yet. In desperation he pushed at Maddy, who fell awkwardly and landed on the rocks with a cry of pain. Tom and Fran rushed to help her. In the meantime, Raymond splashed through the shallow water, Gilbert chasing him and snapping fiercely, and hefted the chests one by one into the boat.

'Looks like you don't have a boat of your own,' he called tauntingly, pushing off and floating out into the cove. 'So, I guess you won't be chasing me!' The tide was going out, and his boat drifted rapidly away from the little beach. Gilbert had to give up the chase and swam back to the beach, shaking himself dry as George appeared over the rocks carrying Raymond's own sopping-wet dog.

'Oh, just one more thing before you escape!' called Maddy, wincing in pain. It felt like her wrist might have broken in the fall.

'What's that then?' called Raymond from his boat. He was certain now that he had got away, even if he had to row all the way to shore.

'You might want to look behind you!'

A large, brand-new boat was floating not far away. It was painted bright blue and white and had the letters KIRRIN POLICE written down the side. Several officers were on board, smiling in satisfaction.

Raymond's face drained of all colour.

'Oh, yes, did we forget to tell you?' yelled Tom, his face lighting up in sheer delight. 'While you were getting the treasure, we borrowed your radio! Hope that's not a problem!'

THREE
MONTHS
LATER

20

Five Are Together Again

Brightly polished and gleaming under the museum
lights, the burial treasures of Whispering Wood were
finally revealed in all their splendour. At the centre of
the display, in its own case, was the ceremonial golden
mask of an ancient queen, richly engraved and
decorated with sparkling gems. Nearby lay her weapons:
an ornate sword and a jewel-encrusted dagger. Bracelets,
necklaces and piles of coins were arranged in different
cases all around the room. A crowd of chattering,
smartly dressed people moved to and fro, gazing in
wonderment at the incredible haul, which hadn't been

seen in more than half a century, since it was stolen and lost in the depths of Kirrin Bay.

'Where's the professor?' Maddy, feeling ill-at-ease in this kind of company, stood on tiptoe to look across the room.

'Relax,' Fran told her. 'George will be here. She promised.'

'What time is the food?' asked Tom. 'The invitation said there'd be canapés. That's just a posh way of saying fancy finger foods, right?' Gilbert gave a small whine at the mention of food.

'There'll be a sausage roll for you, don't worry,' Fran told him with a smile.

Just then there was a stir at the far side of the room. The crowd swirled as a tall figure bustled in. George Kirrin had obviously paid no attention whatsoever to the invitation to this rather glitzy event, least of all the dress code. She was wearing her usual jumper and jeans, with a pair of filthy sneakers that looked as if she used them to do the gardening. George looked around for the three children and gave them a wave of recognition.

She crossed the room towards them, dodging people in smart suits and cocktail dresses. 'I was in the middle of an experiment. I'm—'

'—close to a breakthrough?' Maddy finished for her with a smile.

'Well, yes,' said George, looking confused. 'How did you know?' She cast a glance downwards. 'How's the arm?' she asked Maddy.

'My cast came off a few weeks ago,' the girl replied, rubbing her wrist. 'Good as new.'

'Excellent.' George smiled, looking around the room. 'Where has he got to now?' she went on, before placing two fingers in her mouth and letting out a piercing whistle. The hubbub of polite conversation was stopped dead, not that George cared, or noticed.

A glossy and very well-cared-for dog came trotting through the crowd. His fur was silky, tail held high, and around his neck was an old but spotless leather collar with large, polished metal studs.

'That's the collar from your study!' Fran recognised it straight away. 'And surely that can't be . . . Raymond's poor old dog?'

'He's my dog now,' said George. 'There was no way I was going to let him keep an animal after he threw it into the water. I know he was desperate and terrified. But there's no excuse for that.'

'What's his name?' asked Fran, crouching down to give the happy dog a stroke.

'Timmy Number Two?' suggested Tom.

'There'll never be another Timmy,' George told them sternly. 'But this is Bobs. I swore I'd never have another dog, but somebody had to look after him. Didn't they, boy?' Bobs looked up at her with adoring brown eyes, and the children exchanged delighted smiles.

'Remember when Grandad said he thought this year's summer holiday would be good for all of us?' said Maddy. 'I don't think even he knew how right he was.'

Gilbert leapt forward to greet this new friend, and the two dogs circled each other with a series of delighted barks and much tail-wagging.

Their reunion was interrupted by a gentle *ting ting ting* as somebody tapped a spoon against a champagne glass. The chatter, which had been starting to build again after George's whistle, died away once more. The crowd turned to face a tall, serious-looking woman who was standing beside the case containing the golden mask.

'Welcome,' she announced. 'We are all very privileged to be here, at the first ever public viewing of the Whispering Wood Treasure.' There was a polite smattering of applause. 'For those of you who don't know me,' she went on, 'I am Naya Heath, the Minister for Culture, and I am here on behalf of the Government to celebrate the return of this incredible piece of history. But, most importantly, to pass on the grateful thanks of our whole country to the people who recovered it.'

And now the whole room turned, following the minister's gaze, to stare at Maddy, Fran, Tom and George. Fran felt her face burning with embarrassment, but followed Maddy when Naya Heath said, 'Would you all come up here, please?' The room burst into proper applause and there was a real thunder of appreciation, with cheers and whoops mixed in.

'How long is this going to take?' moaned Tom. 'I'm starving!'

'You really are very much like your Grandad Dick when he was your age,' George told him, placing an arm round his shoulders. 'Come on. If you save a priceless haul of treasure, you've got to deal with a bit of fame.'

'I'd still rather be in the non-famous five,' Tom complained. 'I don't like everyone looking at me.'

'I think you'd better get used to it,' Maddy told him, overhearing.

Even when they had lined up at the front of the hall, the applause and cheering took some time to die down. Eventually the minister had to hold up a hand and silence fell. 'Many of you might already be familiar with Professor George Kirrin,' said Naya, 'through her groundbreaking research into clean energy. With her today are her great-nieces and nephew: Madeleine, Frances and Thomas.'

'And Gilbert,' added Fran with a smile.

'And Bobs!' George reminded her.

The dogs, who seemed to be firm friends already,

both gave a joyful 'Wuff!' and there was a ripple of laughter.

'They thwarted a plot to steal this amazing historical find and take it out of the country,' the minister went on. 'And I am delighted to make two announcements. Firstly – that the Whispering Wood Treasure, after it has been displayed here, will be moved to a brand-new, state-of-the-art museum in Kirrin itself. The professor has been extremely, erm . . . *passionate* in arguing that it should be returned to the place where our ancestors once buried it. And the Government agrees.'

Maddy smiled to herself as another burst of applause washed over them. She could only imagine what a hard time stubborn George must have given the authorities over where to house the treasure. Passionate, she felt sure, was a polite way of saying 'she wouldn't take no for an answer'!

'And secondly,' Naya went on, once the clapping had stopped, 'I am delighted to present all four of you with these special medals for bravery, on behalf of a very grateful nation.' Accompanied by the loudest cheering yet, she handed each of them a slim red box containing a golden medal.

'And that concludes the ceremonial part of the evening,' the minister went on.

'Yes!' Tom punched the air. 'Buffet time!'

There was another wave of laughter which turned gradually into another round of warm applause. The minister rounded things up and invited people to move next door and begin the party.

'Maybe children haven't changed as much as I thought,' said George with a grin, giving Tom's shoulder a quick squeeze as they made their way towards a table filled with food.

Once they had all loaded up their plates they managed to find a space towards the back of the room, away from the crowd.

'I've got so many questions,' said Maddy through a mouthful of sandwich.

'Me too,' said Fran. 'For a start, what's happened to Raymond?'

George gave a small, sad smile. 'He'd been very foolish getting himself mixed up with that man Clay.

I've been doing a bit of digging, with the help of some old friends, and we've found out a bit more about him. His full name is Doctor Cornelius Clay, and he's a very unpleasant man indeed.'

'What old friends?' asked Maddy excitedly, but George seemed not to hear her.

'I agreed not to press charges against Raymond as long as he helped us,' she went on. 'And I think I'm close to tracking down Clay and his gang.'

'So the adventure isn't finished yet?' asked Maddy.

'One adventure might have come to an end,' said George, looking through the doorway at the glass cases full of glittering gold, 'but another one might be about to begin.' The children followed her gaze and caught sight of a woman looking intently at the treasure. She had white hair cut in a neat bob, and when she turned to face them they were met by a pair of kindly, shining eyes with a hint of steel behind them.

'That' – George pointed – 'is one of the people who's been helping me. She's a very famous detective, and her name's A. C. Fox.'

'Cool name,' Tom said admiringly.

The white-haired woman approached them through the milling crowd. 'Hallo,' she said excitedly. 'I haven't seen any of you for a long time, but the professor here has been telling me all about your adventures.'

'Are you really a famous detective?' Maddy wanted to know.

'I don't know about "famous",' said the woman modestly. 'But I am a detective, yes. In fact, I've been helping to solve mysteries for a long time. Isn't that right, George?'

Professor George Kirrin stepped forward and the two of them hugged each other warmly.

'It's so good to see you,' smiled the celebrated detective, A. C. Fox.

'Hallo, Anne,' George replied.

The New Famous Five will return in
FIVE AND THE SMUGGLER'S CODE

Coming soon

Acknowledgements

First of all, thanks to Jenny, Lucas and Mabel – the other members of the Famous Four. Here's to many more adventures! Mabel, you are less brave than Timmy but you need fewer walks.

Thanks to all my fellow authors, especially Anna James, who sternly warned me to 'Do right by Anne!' – I hope you're happy with the last chapter and you're gonna love the next book. And to Kiran Millwood Hargrave for holding a book launch at which I pitched this idea to some startled Hachette people *very* enthusiastically after enjoying several ginger beers.

Enormous thanks to the startled Hachette people in question – Ruth and Harriet. And indeed to everyone at Hachette, especially the wonderful Aliyana, who is the Tinker to my Mischief. We did it!

Massive gratitude to Bhavini for your wonderful design, and James Lancett for bringing the new Five to life so brilliantly.

Stephanie Thwaites, you are just the absolute best. An agent, a friend, a legend. Love you.

To my friend Loo for lending me the very cool name of your very cool dog and for being almost as excited about this story as I was.

To m'colleague Greg James and all Podcastards. Peace, love and more power to your elbows.

Thanks to any people who make cheese and to all pandas.

And thanks to you, if you enjoy reading the acknowledgements. You're my kind of person. Hello!

Meet the
New Famous Five

Maddy

Maddy is the eldest sibling.
She is responsible and a leader and
takes care of her brother and sister.

Fran

Fran is the second eldest.
She always has a serious expression,
but she is very determined and brave.

Tom

Tom is the youngest in the family.
He is very funny and loves food,
especially ice cream.

George

George was part of the original Five.
She is headstrong and courageous,
and hates being called 'Georgina'!

Gilbert

Gilbert is Fran's collie dog who is very
excitable and sweet. He is very protective
of the children when he needs to be.

Chris Smith is a bestselling author and the joint recipient of the 2024 Ruth Rendell Award for his work promoting literacy and campaigning for school libraries. Chris created the *Kid Normal* series with his friend Greg James and recently the pair published *The Twits Next Door* which became an instant bestseller. Chris is also a solo author and has published two fantasy adventures set in his fictional kingdom of Parallelia, including *Frankie Best Hates Quests*.

Before he was an author, Chris worked as a newsreader and presenter on radio stations, including Xfm and BBC Radio 1. His most famous news bulletin is probably the one sampled by George Michael in 1998 and used on his international hit *Outside*. Chris lives in London with his wife Jenny, their son Lucas and Mabel the cat.

James Lancett grew up in Cardiff before moving to London to study BA Illustration and Animation at Kingston University. He now lives in Bath where he works as a bestselling illustrator and animation director, and is known for his illustrations for the *Lenny Lemon* series, the *Adam B* series, Romesh Ranganathan's *Lil' Muffin Drops the Mic* and many others.